Gopal Gandhi took voluntary retirement from the Indian Administrative Service in 1992, was Director of The Nehru Centre, London, from 1992 to 1996, and later High Commissioner for India in South Africa and Sri Lanka, Ambassador of India in Norway, secretary to the President of India and Governor of West Bengal. Gopal (or Gopalkrishna, to use his full name) is married to Tara and they have two married daughters.

If there were to be an anthology of the really worthwhile original Indian plays written since the twentieth century, it would be one of the slimmest books in the world. And Gopal Gandhi's play would occupy pride of place in it. Ever since the merging, so to say, of theatre and cinema in India via the talkies, when all theatrical talent was sucked into the obviously more lucrative cinema, a no-win situation seems to have continuously prevailed in the writing spheres of both cinema and theatre. While in films our screenplay writing has never outgrown the influence of the early talkies and thus of early theatre, the craft of the playwright in our country too has languished and has always seemed to be searching for a direction to evolve in. Gopal Gandhi, by writing this play, has done theatre a double favour. He has provided us with some of the most recitable poetry ever and he has drawn a riveting portrait of the fascinating Dara Shukoh within the framework of a deeply moving story. The writing, while being a sly reminder of the 'grand old' traditions of Indian theatre, is also engagingly modern; the reader will unquestioningly accept the charming anachronisms that appear occasionally. Oh, if only history had been taught to us thus in school!—*Naseeruddin Shah*

What makes Gopal Gandhi's *Dara Shukoh* unique is that it is not just another play about another historical figure but in effect a statement of the author's own philosophy, expressed through the life of a person who tried to embody it but failed—tragically, for the history of India. And the tragedy, vast in its consequences and still reverberating, is expressed in verse, which is admirable for its clarity and control.—*Girish Karnad*

Gopal Gandhi's wonderfully moving and insightful tragedy elegantly and imaginatively revisits one of Indian history's great what-if moments, making us ask again how different things might have been if it was heterodox mystic Dara rather than the puritanical bigot Aurangzeb who had won the civil war and led Mughal India—would Islam and Hinduism have been able to bridge their differences? Would the united Mughal lands have managed to stop the colonial conquests? Would Partition have been impossible? *Dara Shukoh* is a thoughtful and thought-provoking text.—*William Dalrymple*

With love
(signature)
30/12/19

DARA SHUKOH

A Play

GOPAL GANDHI

TRANQUEBAR

TRANQUEBAR PRESS
An imprint of westland ltd
Venkat Towers, 165, P.H. Road, Maduravoyal, Chennai 600 095
No.38/10 (New No.5), Raghava Nagar, New Timber Yard Layout, Bangalore 560 026
Survey No. A-9, II Floor, Moula Ali Industrial Area, Moula Ali, Hyderabad 500 040
23/181, Anand Nagar, Nehru Road, Santacruz East, Mumbai 400 055
47, Brij Mohan Road, Daryaganj, New Delhi 110 002

First published by Banyan Books 1993, a division of the Business India Group of Publications, Mumbai

This edition published by TRANQUEBAR PRESS 2010

Copyright © Gopal Gandhi 2010

All rights reserved

10 9 8 7 6 5 4 3 2 1

ISBN: 978-93-80658-52-0

The painting of Dara Shukoh on the cover is reproduced by permission of The British Library Board, The British Library, Oriental and India Office Collections, 197 Blackfriars Road, London SE1 8NG. The author would like to thank Akhilesh Mithal for drawing his attention to it, and Kapila Vatsyayan, for facilitating access to it.

Typeset in Bell MT by SÜRYA, New Delhi
Printed at Manipal Press Limited

DEDICATED

To the Peri Mahal,
The magical 'Fairies Palace'
Built by Dara Shukoh
On a barely accessible spur
Overlooking Lake Dal
In Srinagar.
Intended by Dara
To be a centre
For the study of celestial bodies,
The magnificent structure
Is now derelict,
Its broken terrace
A reminder of the precariousness
Of lofty visions.

A NOTE FROM THE AUTHOR

Dara's name is spelt in the Roman variously as Dara Shukoh, Dara Shikoh and Dara Shikuh. 'Shikoh' is the more commonly used form but as I have understood the matter from historians and scholars of Persian, 'Shukoh' is the more appropriate spelling as 'Shukoh' means 'glory' in Farsi and 'Shikoh', 'terror'. The Mughal Prince was surely meant to betoken and herald glory. The distinguished biographer of Dara Shukoh, the late Professor Kalikaranjan Qanungo, of Dacca University, has also used 'Shukoh', not 'Shikoh'.

Excerpts from

THE OXFORD HISTORY OF INDIA

By
Vincent A. Smith
(1958 edition)

The four sons of Shahjahan were Dara Shikoh, Shuja, Aurangzeb, and Murad Bakhsh, all men of mature age in 1657, aged respectively 43, 41, 39 and about 33 years. All the four had had considerable experience in military and civil affairs on a large scale. The eldest, who remained with his father, was viceroy of the Punjab and other provinces on the north-west, which he administered through deputies. Shuja ruled the great territories of Bengal and Orissa. Aurangzeb controlled the Deccan, while Murad Bakhsh governed Gujarat and the west . . . All the princes possessed the soldier's virtue of personal valour, which was displayed conspicuously by both Aurangzeb and Murad Bakhsh. Dara Shikoh's considerable natural abilities were neutralized by the violence of his temper and an intolerable arrogance of manner, which gained him hosts of enemies. Shuja, an agreeable man, with some skill as a general, was rendered ineffective by his love of pleasure, and his unreadiness to take instant action at the decisive moment. Murad Bakhsh was a passionate, headstrong, tyrannical man, the bravest of the brave, but drunken, dissolute and brainless. It is needless to draw a formal sketch of the character of Aurangzeb, whose consummate ability as an unscrupulous intriguer and cool politician is apparent on the face of the narrative. Although his failures in Balkh and at Qandahar may be regarded disparaging to his skill as a commander of armies, his imperturbable self-possession enabled him to emerge with success from most embarrassing tactical situations during the war of succession. His indomitable resolve to win the throne at any cost and by any means carried him through and gave him victory.

The unorthodoxy of Dara Shikoh was an important factor in the struggle. That prince, while continuing to conform to the Sunni ritual and to be a professed Muslim of the Hanafi school, was deeply imbued with the pantheistic mysticism of the Sufis. He also associated gladly with Hindu philosophers ... He was so intimate with Father Busee and other priests that he was believed by some persons to be within measurable distance of embracing Christianity. That attitude towards Islam infuriated Aurangzeb, who certainly was a devout Sunni Muslim, whatever judgment may be formed of his moral character. He regarded his eldest brother as a pestilent infidel, deserving of worse than death.

(By permission of
Oxford University Press)

ACT ONE

Shahjehanabad, Delhi. The Imperial capital's exclusive sector, where the Red Fort and other mansions of the aristocracy are located.

SCENE 1

The Red Fort's Diwan-i-Khas, the Hall of Special Audiences. A throne is positioned at the centre. Carpets, cushions are spread on the floor. Six liveried heralds are on duty. A herald near the left entrance sounds the bugle which alerts other heralds and sends some half a dozen women (behind a grilled alcove to the side of the throne) into a shiver of nervous excitement. Shah Jehan, the Moghul emperor, is about to enter this exclusive chamber in his palace.

Herald   [Loudly, for everyone in the Hall

Witness! with a measured pace
His Royal Majesty arrives!
To feel his sandals, trimmed with lace,
Each gleaming marble floor-tile vies!

Second Herald   [Equally loud

Behold the royal countenance!
Allah has fashioned it—
Giving the Earth a radiance
The sun can scarce requit.

1

Female Attendant   [*From the alcove, almost swooning*

He comes, he comes, the badshah comes!
My heart he ignites, my feet benumbs!

Second Female Attendant   [*Stern-facedly, under her breath*

Don't let Princess Roshanara
Catch you in euphoria.

First Female Attendant

Killjoy princess, killjoy you!
Go drown yourself, you parvenu!

First Herald   [*To second Herald, dropping his voice*

Yesterday, on elephant back
At the great mosque, did you glimpse
The King scatter from his velvet sack
Gold, in rich munificence?

Second Herald

Indeed I did, and also saw
Our goodly prince Dara Shukoh
Command at once such love and awe
As would incense his wily foe.

First Herald

Not so loud, friend, not so loud,
The Deccan has ears in these walls.
A spy in every south-bound cloud
Carries tales from Delhi's halls.

Second Herald

I know that well. I can see it:
This court's a traphouse of intrigue
Where rumour, envy and deceit
Are all in sweet-talking league.
Power, leverage, spell and sway
Everyone propitiates.
If one has a fine to pay
But not the means, he insinuates
A present into his salaam,
And can contrive from the rear
A waiver by the warmed palm.
Why, Jean Baptiste Tavernier
Himself must transact business
In court by lubric exertions.
And 'look after' with finesse
Its unembarrassed minions!

First Herald

How right you are, my good friend!
This place thrives on lubricity.
Here you will see vassals bend
Low with sick mendacity
Before some strutting courtier:
'Will you please put in a word
To our magnific vizier
Whose counsel and insights are heard
By our King enchantedly?'
The very wretch will then glide
Towards the rivals, abjectly,
'Nobles on our Prince's side,
Pray, this Nobody, patronize,'

And looking over his shoulder
Whisper ... *'In a wicked enterprise*
Like Sher Khan's, only bolder,
The vizier's men at Abu
Have planned a daring coup ... '

Second Herald

And thus foment Dara's mind
To provocation ever inclined.

> *[In the other corner of the hall,*
> *Third Herald speaks, moving*
> *towards Fourth Herald*

Third Herald

Have you noticed those two mumbling
Constantly to each other?
I can tell you, their grumbling
Is not about the weather.

Fourth Herald   *[In a whisper, with teeth clenched*

They're clearly of Dara's party,
I've named them: Sharp and Smarty.
Prince Aurangzeb will hear of this,
With a swelling of irises
And Mir Jumla, made wise,
Will serve them a nasty surprise.

First Herald

There, the Emperor's now seen!
He inclines a bejewelled ear
Towards his windbag vizier,
And makes that rascal preen.

First Female Attendant [*Swaying*

Hush! My Imperial Majesty nears!
His limbs to caress, the curtain veers.
His every footstep the carpet hugs,
Each straining knot, a tassel tugs.

Second Female Attendant

Be still, you dizzying dreamhead,
You fluttering bi-ped.
Display your nervous tension
When all his attention
Is yours; when washed, refreshed, he dines
Or later, heavy-lidded, reclines
Contemplating the curl
Of some new-got slave-girl.
Not here! This is the Diwan-i-Khas
Not the place to swing your. . . .

Third Female Attendant

There comes Dara, mystic prince,
Every damsel heart he wins.
Do you know of royal eyes
Like his which can mesmerize?

[*The Emperor enters, with
Dara Shukoh, Sadullah Khan,
some noblemen and attendants.
They are engaged in banter.
Shah Jehan seats himself on the
throne*

Shah Jehan

So how, my vizier,
Do our crops appear;
How does the inflow
Of revenues go?

Sadullah

My Emperor, most kind,
Tonight, before you've dined,
I will show you the sheets
Of our State receipts
Takings, rents, taxes, fines,
Profits gained from our mines.
And by dawn, before
You rise, I will have more
Reports on the reasons
Why, despite the season's
Being good, collections
Trail expectations.

Shah Jehan

Thank you my good vizier
That will make it easier . . .

Dara

Majesty, forgive me please
For thus interrupting you.
The vizier has won a lease
Of time, just to bamboozle you!

Shah Jehan

Haughty Prince Dara,
Naughty Prince Dara!

Dara

You asked if the crops were good
To know where the coffers stood.
He must say they are all right
Or are not, so the court might
Consider what is proper, wise:
Peace—or some fool enterprise
To annex yet more acreage
By ploy, perfidy, pillage.

Sadullah   *[Clearing his throat*

My young prince is, well, young,
Gives his mind a ready tongue.
But, Majesty, I'm older
Slower, an upholder
Of the dictum: speak not
Half-bake, lest you be caught
(Like a feline's useless runt)
In a pair of mother jaws
Executing nature's laws.

Dara

Diplomatic softspeak,
Can muffle conspiracy's creak
Working to subvert this throne
By means known and unknown.

*[Sadullah appears provoked and
starts to speak, but the Emperor
gestures to calm him down*

Shah Jehan

Son, aren't you being hasty,
Unfair, or just feisty
When you say the vizier
Dissimulates here?
Sound advice in his aim
He has no deeper game.

> *[The princesses Jahanara and*
> *Roshanara appear at the alcove.*
> *Roshanara sits behind the grille,*
> *while Jahanara remains*
> *standing, listening attentively,*
> *as Dara speaks*

Dara

Their game is to seal the fate
—And before it is too late—
Of those of us here
Who stand for India.
And of those who wish to make
Of our royal line, no fake
'Heavenly Protectorate'
But a truly inviolate
Agency for human good
As part of a larger Godhood.
They'll use every manoeuvre
To try pull the wool over
Your eyes, as they draw up their plan,
With all the devilry of Man,
To manipulate the course
By stealth first, and then by force,

Of our royal lineage.
That is why, father, I rage.

Shah Jehan

I have known of your rage—
When I was your age
My father knew of mine!
It's so with every line
Of rulers dynastic.
A fancy fantastic
Drives them all to fury,
Doing some injury
Sometimes, but often good.
And if I've understood
Your own rage correctly,
And contextually,
Indignation's the name.
You suspect a game
To overthrow this court
And install in the Fort
An order which will freeze
Akbar's tolerant decrees
And use my indulgences
Of the five known senses,
To, themselves, the sixth use
A proper time to choose
For a usurpation
Of this royal station.

*[Sadullah tenses, while
Dara seems appeased*

Dara

Father, you've spoken my mind,
In words I couldn't hope to find.

Shah Jehan   [*Addressing all those present*

Dara hates bigotry
He wants faiths to be free
And encouraged to preach
Concordance each to each,
He sees for himself here
A role that goes near
Akbar's, minus the crown.
And when he sees this drown
In courtcraft's slurry
He cannot but worry!
Yet Dara, be assured,
Your fears will be cured.

Here's a proclamation:
No one's machination
Will shake the Peacock Throne.
If anyone be prone
To tricks or subterfuge
He'll pay a price, so huge
As to rue the evil day
He went foul treason's way.

[*Sadullah is now in
consternation and starts to speak,
but the Emperor again prevents
him*

That should satisfy you,
Dara! Nor displease true,

Good, Sadullah.' Now
Tell me, vizier, how
Our inlayers-in-charge,
Have embellished the Taj-
The pure marble bare
I know, is past compare,
But the 'finishing touches'
Put our targets in crutches!

Sadullah

Most benign Emperor,
Art's unique connoisseur!
I was there the other day
To see if the inlay
Being done on the grave
And the front architrave
Would clash with the marble
And so doing, garble
The vault's lucent message.
But no, edge rivals edge.

A painter using dew
And fresh pollen in lieu
Of tincts: a lucid night's
Bespangled stars for whites
And the sky for his blues
Would envy the lambent hues
Our inlayers create.
The grooves they now striate
See gem blending with stone
And shape fusing with tone.

Shah Jehan   *[With eyes glazed in reverie*

I wish to create
Art so immaculate
As will set a standard
By craft to be pandered
For an eternity
Of emmarbled beauty.
The Taj, through moonlight strobes,
(Like a nymph who disrobes
But keeps her ornaments)
In all her adornments

[Dara looks at his father,
disapprovingly

Will flash in lunar light:
Now blue, now white.

Forgive that image, son,
You know my interests run
On three paths: gems, buildings
And that passion of kings
I need not name. I choose
All three well made, refuse
Those that aren't. All three should
Be, seem, and feel, good.
I know you disapprove
Of my simile; view
Erotics with distaste.
Let that picture go waste.

I will try another,
Worthier of your mother:
Time's silent oyster-womb

Will, in its hidden room
With gentle love, fashion
A pearl of perfection
So it shall ever rest
Unflawed, on Sorrow's breast,
Transporting some future
Bard to say in rapture,
'This monument sublime
Is the Tear of Time.'

Sadullah   *[In an aside*

He wanders in his daydreams
While my papers grow by reams!

I must now change my accents,
My rhythms, metre, and song.
And ensure that he attends
To business which mustn't prolong.

[Addressing the Emperor

Majesty, may I assure
You: that lustrous monument,
That white masterpiece so pure,
Writes your name on Time's parchment?

Shah Jehan

Your kind reassurance
Does me good, faithful friend,
For I now often glance
At the shadows which extend
On the stern sundial
Of my life. Time holds it
In both hands—my phial

Of wine—and drains it.
He drinks me to the lees.
I'm 'aged', if you please!
I have to now prepare
For that final journey
To which God does not spare
Men for your company.
I've to go to that shore
Where no one is 'common',
No one King, any more.
And, jobless, lies Mammon.

Jahanara   [*She rises to speak from the
                              alcove. Princess Roshanara
                              continues sitting and looks away
                              as her elder sister begins*

Father, speak not in that strain.
It causes such pain
As I can neither express
Nor try to suppress
In the pulse of my fear
Or a withheld tear.
You can recall, I am sure.
Sixteen forty-four,
When my fine muslin attire
Touched a lamp, caught fire
And two maids saving me, died.
You stayed at my side
And for my flickering life, prayed
Till I was spared.
And so I cannot bear to see.
You in mind of death. For me
More hangs by your life, Father,
Than heaven and earth together.

Roshanara   [*Disdainingly*

Just this hangs by a King's life:
At his waist, a knife.
Without it the crown he wears
Is a load he bears—
No better than a dumb milkmaid's.
And so the good blade's
Transference on his demise,
Must be very wise ...

Dara   [*Quaking with rage*

She insults you, Father, she does.
How dare she speak to you thus?
You are her father, her King.
No child she is schooling!
'His demise', what does she mean?
Father, ask her to come clean.
This concept of 'knife' I refute
Totally, I also impute
A motive, both mean and low
To her and to her fellow ...

Roshanara

I was talking to him;
Stop being so dim!

Dara   [*Almost choking*

'Him?' 'Dim?' Just how can you dare?
He's the King, and don't you glare
At me like that, understand?
I know the venom of your brand

15

And its antidote as well
Which can consign you to hell.

*[Dara moves to a corner and
leans against a wall emotionally
drained and, after a minute,
begins to soliloquize. A spotlight
rests on him as the others continue
to prattle inaudibly*

Dara

Princess Roshanara,
I was once so fond of you!
Your once-loved Prince Dara.
O woe, that now you view
My friends as your foes, and my
Foes as friends. I can't bear this
Transformation of a shy
Sister's breath into a hiss.
But there's ambition for you!
The finest natures it can taint
And make them break the queue
Of natural restraint.

*[The spotlight goes out. The
Emperor begins to rise from his
throne, when his vizier speaks.
He holds on official document in
his hand, given to him by an
attendant. The Emperor resumes
his seat*

Sadullah

There is one little matter left
Which, If Your Majesty permits,
I could just mention in the weft,
So to say. A prisoner sits,
Outside: Jiwan Khan from Multan.
He is charged with plotting treason
And planning to become a sultan,
(Would you believe it?) this season
Of figs. The evidence is strong
Against him; the defence, weak.
It will not take the court long
To establish guilt and seek
Your Majesty's decision
On the Governor's petition.

Shah Jehan   *[Taking his hand to his eye*

My eyelid has a flutter
Does Fate some warning utter?

Sadullah   *[Moving, with quick-reflex*
                             solicitude, towards the Emperor

My wife makes an ointment
For the eyes. An unguent ...

Shah Jehan   *[Reverting to business*

This matter should have come
Before me at the 'Am
Not here at the 'Khas.
Never mind; let that pass.

*[Sadullah, in embarrassment,
seeks to apologize but the
Emperor continues*

I've decided. The rogue
Must get what is in vogue
For crimes against the State:
The elephant's dire weight
Upon his scheming head,
Till he is pronounced dead.
Then, tied to the beast's tail
The corpse will regale
The people of Delhi
As 'Treachery's Folly'.
We do not countenance
The slightest insouciance
From the likes of this man,
Golcondan or Afghan.

*[Sadullah bows gratefully and
drops the document into the
attendant's hand. An elegant
disposal! Shah Jehan rises,
looking towards the female
attendants in the alcove.*

Now! for some well-earned rest
In a soft, feathered nest.

Dara

If the vizier thinks he can
Make this court dance to his score
He is in error. His plan
Can go flying on this floor!

Father, I have something to say
In this case of Malik Jiwan.

> *[Shah Jehan, a trifle irritated,*
> *sits down*

Before the sun has set today
Your sworn enemies would have won.

Shah Jehan

Enemies I have none
But one, my son, but one.

Dara

But one *son*, father, one son!
And he it is who's won.

> *[Sadullah and Roshanara*
> *exchange glances and Roshanara*
> *rises to protest*

Shah Jehan

My one enemy
Is loneliness. It grips me.
It drives me to commit
Excesses or omit
Some important action,
Preferring the distraction
Of Mumtaz in my dream
Or of my choice harim.

Dara   [*After a pause when he seems to
be collecting his thoughts*

Malik Jiwan's, I am told,
Is the kind of vassalage:
Quick-muscled, gallant, bold
Which gets termed as 'brigandage'.
Some people would like to play
On your brusque approach to law
And shape your thoughts like clay
Toys. They'll turn into an outlaw
Him who will not conspire
With them to subvert this throne.
All that Jiwan did aspire
Was some acreage of his own.
We could have counted on
Jiwan to then utilize
It as a buffer, not a pawn
On the chessboard of enterprise.
But honey-talk, not honesty
Works here. In a few hours
We will watch truth's travesty
Enacted. One who towers
In his homeland as Delhi's
Soldier will by Delhi's fiat
Be trampled—with what ease!—
Under four elephant feet.

Delhi, Agra and Lahore
May be our empire's hard core.
But then we have rimlands
Of soft snow and softer sands,
Which need gentle handling
Care and understanding.

We cannot hold our borders
On the strength of Court Orders!
Maps aren't just glued-up charts
They're a protocol of hearts
—And minds—like Jiwan Khan's
And Emperor Shah Jehan's.
Forgive him, Father; free him, King.

[Roshanara is visibly agitated

Let us make a fresh beginning.

Shah Jehan

Beside your obiter
(Which offends your sister)
There's much in what you say
On the matter per se.
'Loyal' and 'disloyal'
Are but adjectival
Prefixes. Much can rest
On who applies the test.

If the Crown Prince thinks so
I cannot just say 'No
Go on, execute him.'
My heart says 'Release him,'
My head, the opposite.
But then your plea does it.
He is free, your Afghan,
To go home, a free man.

[Sadullah stands transfixed.
Dara bows. Shah Jehan rises
and departs. The Court disperses.
Roshanara lingers at the alcove
and buttonholes Sadullah

Sadullah [*In an aside*

Lord! There comes the daughter
Turning my blood to water!

Roshanara

The King has overruled
You, for Dara has fooled
The King. But despair
Not. This you can repair
Soon enough, provided
You are by him guided
Who rules the Deccan, nimbly
Today and will—Insh-Allah—Delhi!

But to change the subject
To—my garden project.
Most noble vizier!
The Frenchman, Bernier,
I am told, has a flower
With teeth that can devour
Insects; also rare seeds
From France. My garden needs
New blood (as does the State!).
Soft, namby flowers grate
On my nerves. Rainbow hues,
Those golds and sky blues
Sicken me. I would like
The smart Frenchman to spike
His manure with acids
Which will burn the flaccids
In their seed-roots to make
Them yield, for my sake,
Freak petals, and very bitter,
Black, styptic nectar.

Sadullah

Please rest assured, Princess,
Your word is 'State Business'!
I will get through to him
With all dispatch and vim.

> *[Roshanara leaves. Sadullah, the
> heralds and attendants, both male
> and female, converge into a
> group. They chant in chorus*

Sadullah

We are nameless
    Civil Servants,
We are blameless
    Civil Servants!

All

We are blameless
    Civil Servants!

Sadullah

We take no sides,
    We Civil Servants.
Let him who rides
    Us, Civil Servants,
Ride us, chide us, bully us,
    Servants
Punctilious (though bilious!)
    Servants.

We never flatter,
We Civil Servants.
We but serve a platter—
Of Gems for their sarcophagi,
Unguents for the eye!

All

Gems for their sarcophagi,
Unguents for the eye!

Sadullah

And besides the nitty-gritty
        We possess—integrity!

All

We possess—integrity!

> [*Many heralds and attendants
> take out necklaces, cash pouches
> and suchlike from their pockets,
> putting them back with a wink*

Sadullah

We have ac-ui-ty,
        Servants,
We give con-tin-uity!
We give con-tin-uity!

We bear no malice,
        Civil Servants,
We drink deep the chalice.
What if it be poisoned,
        Servants,

What if it be poisoned?
What if *I* mayn't stay alive,
Our *species* will survive!

All   [*They troop out, chanting the
                                            refrain*

Yes!
Our species will survive!
We are nameless
    Civil Servants,
We are blameless
    Civil Servants. . . .

SCENE II

*It is late afternoon, the following week, at Prince Dara's
mansion, Delhi. Dara is seated in his private room, on the
floor, in front of a low sloping desk. He is writing. Dara's
companion, Jester, is watching the prince at work.*

Jester

Pondering, reading, writing
All, except being Prince.
Eldest son of the mighty King
Will your learning ever convince
Anyone of your ability
To rule India as it should
Be ruled: with spunk and celerity
Or—as Aurangzeb would?

Dara

Jester mine, you jest on;
That's your nature, calling, skill.

25

While I on Fate's road quest on,
A trusting servant of Allah's will.

Jester

Now that's where you baffle me.
Are you Prince or Saint?
Must you for all time be
At once, a 'may' *and* 'mayn't'.?
Make up your mind now: sage or
Soldier; a seer
Or ruler, but not both. For
God's sake, be clear!

Dara   *[Looking out of a window*

There is no doubt in *my* mind.
My pattern is well defined.
Babur laid the foundation
For our future nation;
Humayun saved it from marauders
Within and beyond its borders.
Then Akbar built in granite brick
Stalwart walls, elephant thick,
To withstand siege, storm or quake
Which none but God could shake.
A strength that came not from rock
Or some man-excluding lock
But from the versatility
Of Hindostan's plurality.
Jehangir made the howdah
Of statehood even prouder
By a measured ostentation
Which my father's celebration
Of power has finally crowned.

But this elation can be drowned
In the Lake of Narcissus
Unless—may God help us—
We begin to see ourselves
Not just as dynastic shelves
In a stately cabinet
But as the legitimate
Heirs of a Higher Will meant
To found more than a government:
A Wider Kingdom, lofty, grand,
In this many-rivered land
Where, awash and self-renewed,
India is from herself rescued,
And where man with man and nature
Comes to acquire his true stature.

Jester

Hold it, you Prince-cum-Moses,
Give me wisdom in smaller doses!

Dara

India needs a thinker
On the Peacock Throne.
A thinker, who will link her
With creation's ozone,
Who will proclaim an 'ilahi'
Greater than ever thought of yet,
Not for a better badshahi
But a re-defined badshahyat
That will transform Delhi's ruler
From a sway-sozzled, lusty
King of varying demeanor
Into India's First Trustee.

27

I can see I will rule;
I will rule, I see.
I am not the fool
You take me to be.
India needs a scholar
On the Peacock Throne.
Anyone who is smaller.
That seat will now disown.

Jester   [*Miming every sentence*

Ho! a bookworm on the glittering
Couch, lost amid its emerald posts,
Pearly curves and rainbow-scattering
Diamond rays. Your peacock hosts
Are tickled, but not for long. Angered,
They train on you their ruby eyes:
'Out, you creepy, crawly fish-turd,
Out!' and quake their tail-sapphires
In a paroxysm of rage at you.
But you, of course, are not to be rushed.
Only when their enamelled beaks spew
Fire, do you see you have trespassed.

Dara

I know I will ascend
The Peacock Throne one day.
So why should I pretend
To be another lay
Aspirant: jealous, sly,
Vengeful? I know, of course,
That my brothers will try
And are trying, to force
Their way to what is mine

28

By right—I am eldest.
But quite apart from Line,
There is another test:
I am—Allah be praised—
Truly—trusted by all.
Frankly, I am amazed

[A knock is heard

To see ... Did someone call?

*[Jester goes out to find who has
knocked. In the meantime, Dara
stands up and soliloquizes*

Why do you assure me,
Lord, of infinite Grace,
And tell me Destiny
Has kept a special place
For me and yet give no
Sign of any such thing?
Should you not sometimes show
Me proof that I will be King?

Jester   *[Jester returning*

Khan Malik Jiwan is here
With mules bearing
Gifts, to see you. I fear
He's in a most tearing
Hurry. Saying he must meet
You and 'place his salaam
At your exalted feet'
He's promptly warmed my palm!

Dara

Then you must have held it out, you tease,
And, of course, you'll blame the times!
I'll meet him: bring him in please.
Good luck requits his crimes.

> *[Jester goes out and returns with*
> *Malik Jiwan Khan, who falls at*
> *Dara's feet.*

Dara

Rise, brave Pathan
My good Afghan!

Jiwan   *[Half rising*

I cannot look you in the eye;
You are Allah's voice for me
I will serve you till I die;
My soldiers are your army.

Dara

Rise, good friend. A silver rift

> *[Jiwan rises and stands*
> *respectfully*

In your cloud of misfortune
Has let in life's greatest gift
To man: contrition, hewn
Out of guilt. I knew, Jiwan,
You were not guiltless. I knew
Of your violent acts. But one
Thing stood out in all that you

Did: You were no manipulator.
Angered, you could be vicious
But never turn conspirator.
That's why they grew suspicious.

Jiwan

My Prince, my benefactor,
You are right. There is much
That I must atone for.
But if they as much as touch
You, Prince, they will have to reckon
With Jiwan Khan, the Pathan
Whose soldiers will take them on,
In open battle at Multan.

Dara

I know that, Jiwan, know it well.
And thank you for your loyalty.
Insh-Allah all will go well
With this line of royalty.
But give up carnage, please,
It is sheer insanity.
Now, go; may your tribe increase
In God' magnanimity.

[*Jiwan bows and turns to go*

Jester

And the gifts, Prince, can we keep them
Too, in God's magnanimity?
The Khan has given me a gem
I think, in sheer sanity.

*[Jiwan, without waiting for
Dara's reply, leaves. Another
knock is heard. Jester goes to
check. Dara soliloquizes again*

Dara

More visitors! And not one verse
Have I done into Persian
Today. Sanskrit is taut, terse,
Like tightly coiled hessian
String. I will not percisize
Its thrift with sound, not try
Change its original guise.
I will not, with Khayyam, vie.

*[Jester returns with
Kavindracharya Saraswati*

Acharj! You are well-arrived.
I was reading the *Geet*.
Help me, learned friend, decide
What meaning is more meet
For this stanza: 'Whenever

*[The Acharya sits down beside
Dara, listening*

Dharma declines, O Bharat,
(And this will be true forever)
I will myself body forth?'
Now 'Bharat', you have explained,
Stands for 'Arjun'; so 'O Bharat'
Is 'O Arjun'. And yet, declaimed,
I feel they mean by 'Bharat'

No person, but 'India'.
The Lord promises our nation
Succour when evil reigns here
And the good are in desperation.

Jester

Doubtless you see yourself, chariot-
Borne, a discus swirling in your
Hand; a Krishna on the quiet!
But, no. You can't as much as ensure. . . .

Dara

Shush! Enough of your jesting.
The Acharj does not have time
For it. Forgive my suggesting

[Turning to Acharya

A version which might not rhyme
With yours. But then that's Sanskrit!
See a word so, and it will denote
This; but so, and the word will fit
An altogether new coat.

Arjun's doubt plagues India;
All of us have sinned here.
Who's so blameless as to blame?
Who, from guilt, can exemption claim?

Either through the April haze,
We see a truant moon to spy,
Or bethreaded, at Kasi, praise
The virtues of the sun and sky.
All of us will bathe and swathe
Then expatiate on Faith.

Yet at Help's threshold we'll linger.
And when someone's in distress,
For fear of soiling a little finger,
To More Urgent Business we'll press.

Kavindrachrya

I'm supposed to be a pandit
But more 'spirituality'—
I wouldn't recommend it.
We need more humanity!
Plain scholarship is just effete
When the need is for action.
Of Thought, we have a surfeit,
Of human care, a fraction.
And *that's* confined to our own kind,
To our own interest.
Is never inclined
To think for the Rest.
In fact we travel further,
On the road to cleavage:
Each other we'll murder,
Destroy hut and tillage
In the name of religion
And of Otherness.
We're but duck and widgeon,
But lord, the bitterness!

That's why India's in decline.
'Dharma' must not incline
To idle contemplation
But opt for intervention.
On the wages of mutual neglect
(And worse) we must all reflect.
All of us have this weakness:

We deny others' sacredness.
Denying it, we then kill
And use the blood we spill
In a sick libation of our
Own altars to inveigle power.
The price of millennial decay
Let us all now prepare to pay.
It is time we revised taboos,
Time we erased tattoos.
India can well replace
Arjun, and invoke His grace.

Jester   [*Interrupting Kavindracharya*

But tell me Acharj please, will not
This avtarhood unleash never-
Ending combat: A 'good' plot
Against a 'bad', a high fever
That wracks the body
Before leaving it dead?

Will India be a Tragedy
For God to read in bed?

Kavindracharya

That's not the Song's longer aim,
Eternal combat's not the name
Of its purpose. It is really
The opposite: To finally
End, not enemies but enmity
And seek, with humility
And love to befriend the foe
Making of arrow and bow
—Kaurav weapons of treachery—
Mere instrument of archery.

35

Dara

I wish I could see the day
When my foes brothers become
Or that I could see my way
To ... Insh-Allah the day will come!
In the meantime, tell me friend,
How things fare at Varanasi;
Has the infamous head-rent
Been waived or is Delhi fussy?

Kavindracharya

I could not meet the vizier
To tell him how the jizya
Is by all of us just—hated!
We feel so humiliated
At having to pay this tax
And that to a State so lax
About human security.
In Prayag's vicinity
Crime and rapine in the fiefs
Are perpetrated by—bailiffs!
Their malignant zest
Clips crime to self-interest.
Patronage can hush a murder
And ugly mayhem, launder.

Dara

When will this anarchy end,
Order from disorder rise;
When will you, O Lord, extend
To us the mercy of your eyes?

Jester

When you cease soliloquizing
That's when! Cease being a poet
Ever romanticizing
Life, instead of being alert.
Take my advice: By one swift swerve
Swat your foes, so they can't revive.
Even God would need some nerve
In India to survive!

> [*Another knock is heard and
> Jester goes out*

Dara

Ignore him, please, Acharj, Jester
Means well. He jolts me out of
Self-pity. Though a waster
Of precious time he is, of
Time he is also a symbol:
He gives me chance after chance
To measure up to the label
'Prince' but threatens change of stance
At will; he lives on a pittance;
Stays more for love. I will
Never give him quittance,
The laughing, scoffing, devil!

> [*Jester returns with Niccolao
> Manucci*

Manucci

My prince Dara! Do I intrude
Upon some contemplative
Work, with my rather crude
And unimaginative
Arrival? I see the Acharj
Is here and must beg his
Pardon, too. But there is at large
A rumour which to your notice. . . .

*[Dara rises and goes with
Manucci to a corner,
Kavindracharya begins to read a
manuscript which lies on the
floor. A spotlight falls on Jester,
dimming the others from view.
Jester speaks to the audience*

Jester

He thinks I'm here for love, he does.
    That's but half the story.
Witnessing is more my purpose,
    Witnessing tragedy.
I often cry when he siestas,
    Though weeping's not my line.
Dara will never know that Jester's
    Eyes can brim with brine.

Manucci holds the prince urbane,
    Gracious, compassionate.
And so he is. But far too vain
    To quite appreciate

Frank advice. He's always polite
       To his friends but can turn
Abusive at the very sight
       Of knaves Fate does not spurn.

A latitudinarian,
       Dara can be narrow-
Tempered! A complex Hadrian,
       In mood, muscle, marrow,
He can also be very naïve!
       He wears a Hindu ring
And promptly sends a whole beehive
       Of objections, buzzing.
They don't know Dara who speaks thus
       And may well think this odd:
Dara's unlike the rest of us:
       He has experienced God.

> *[The spotlight goes off, the stage*
> *is re-lit and the focus returns to*
> *where Dara and Manucci have*
> *been talking*

Manucci

So that's what I've heard, my master
Heard it at the gunnery,
That Mir Jumla having amassed
Men and muskets, there's no worry
Any more, about Golconda.
He's sure to be raised to Five
Thousand and I won't wonder
If he's made a minister, why,
Chief minister, if the mission

Succeeds. But more sinister, sires,
A grander designation
Tempts him whom Jumla inspires,
And him who trusts Jumla now:
To fetch Deccani gem and stone
And enjewel, with his knowhow,
The climb to the Peacock Throne.

Dara

Thank you my friend, I will speak
To my father; speak to him today.
I'll tell him not to be so weak
As to let treason get away.
For treason's what this is, this rifling
Of the South, despite clear
Orders that we should do nothing
That might occasion fear.

Aurangzeb's blinded by wealth,
By pastures that aren't his own.
Tiptoeing, with hyena stealth,
He springs on sinless fawn.

> *⌈The muezzin is heard.*
> *Kavindracharya and Manucci*
> *withdraw, bowing*

Dara

Its time for prayer, I find.
Go fetch the princess, Jester dear,
Since yesterday, she hasn't dined,
Quaking with some nameless fear.

> *⌈As Jester leaves, Dara begins*
> *another self-colloquy*

Nadira, India's future queen,
There's nothing to be afraid of.
The voyage is done; the shore, seen
Our canoe has touched the wharf.

[*Nadira enters*

Nadira

I will be with you, always, Dara,
But, tell me, should we not amend
Being King as your One End
Or my wearing a queen's tiara?

Ambition's fatal, prince, even
In those by custom anointed
As you are, and appointed
To conserve a line, by Heaven.

It's not that I some dream have seen
(Trust me, I have no paranoia)
But two days back a falcon here
Spied and grabbed my pet ermine.

Nature permits such an exit,
But we'd grown fond of each other!
It went screeching into ether,
While I did nothing to help it.

Ever since then I keep seeing
Our sons torn from us by falcons
Borne away, screaming, on talons
Leaving us dazed, disbelieving.

What is there in being king?
The crown's a bauble, power specious.

Our children are what's truly precious;
Let us to their heartbeats, cling.

Dara

Don't read into Nature's cycle.
Lamb in leopard jaws, lambkin
In serpent bind; be literal.
There is, in life, no 'lose or win'.
We just fulfill our destiny.
Do you the sly gecko reproach
For slinking out of its cranny
And terminating a roach?

In our exquisite album
The studies of bird and flower
Reveal an equilibrium
Twist those that do and don't devour.

Take our divine Peri Mahal
Mist-veiled, in Sirinagar,
That monument ethereal
Which overlooks the Dal from a spur.

Within the lake's placid waters
Murders take place by the minute.
Fish eat fish; are eaten by otters.
Violence marks every thing in it.

Nature cleanses, scavenges,
Puts things in place. And, so doing,
All contrariness, balances.
Join karma to this proceeding,
And you have a deeper perspective!
Our own conduct has been guiltless,
That of our foes, most defective.

We should be safe; don't be listless.
You have been under stress, princess
But are bound to feel better
When, in your sacred prayer recess
You commune with our Begetter.

[The call to prayer is heard as
the curtain comes down

SCENE III

*An evening some months thereafter, at Niccolas Manucci's
lodgings. The Venetian entertains Jean Baptiste Tavernier
and Father Busee. The parlour has some western style furniture,
although the windows and doors suggest a typical building in
Shahjehanabad. A large drawing of Mary and the child Jesus
adorns the main wall.*

Manucci

To keep his ageing spirits young,
On his harim's jasper wall
Shah Jehan has had mirrors hung
Which reflect and repeat a voile's fall
From the dancer's face and shoulder
In a hundred multiplying frames,
Tantalizing the beholder.
And then the chandelier flames
As its droplets miniaturize
The swirling form and, like a Jury,
Her gesture, movement, mood, assize.
I've seen there, Kathak danced in fury
To such beat of feet as would alarm
Spain's best tapdancer into retreat:

Thaam-tha-thaam-thaam-thaaam!
I've never known dance to raise such heat.

Busee

I sometimes wonder how it is
That Prince Dara has survived
The vibrations harims release
Slyly, into the lion's pride.
It's not just that he sides
A regime of wise continence
But that he delights
In a *superior* Dalliance.
A Jesuit knows but one meaning
Of that mystic word: 'rapture'.
I had a plan of binding
This (with some sufi ligature)
To Dara's religious baggage.
But, I found, there was no need to!
He knew each chapter and passage
Of the New Testament and so
Taught me, instead, the true purport
And conveyance of Christ's Passion.
Prince Dara's studies to support
With converse, is now my mission.

Manucci

I know what you mean, Father,
Dara is a slave of God.
A philosopher-prince, rather
Than a pea with peas in a pod.
That's why I've chosen to join
His service. He's no employer,
But mentor; no dumb duke but doyen

Of civilized behaviour.
He reminds me, spontaneous,
Of Rome's philosopher-king
Brave Marcus Aurelius
Who governed, meditating.

Busee

A somewhat kindred thing
I have heard from Bernier:
Once Aurangzeb, while fighting,
In battle-smoke, sat down to prayer
Unafraid of the leaden rain
That fell about him unabated.
One would have thought him insane.
He was not; just insulated.

Tavernier

I am no philosopher
Nor even too educated;
I cannot with Bernier
Or Father Busee be rated.
But my long experience
With buyers of precious stones
Has afforded me the chance
To observe human *tones*.
I have come to know the Shah
Of Persia, and the Moghul
Court. I must say that by far
The noblest, truly regal
Of all the lords I have met
Is Dara Shukoh. Regal is
That regal does. I try to get
A present or two for his

Minions but he will not himself
Receive without giving double.
When I gave him a four-door shelf
He responded with a crystal!
While other nobles' sole interest
Lies in prices to bargain,
Dara asks how an amethyst
Differs from sapphire and again
How a pearl of lively waters
Perfectly round and transparent
Would in knowledgeable quarters,
Rank with one of higher carat.

Manucci

When I first reached his presence
I offered my most practiced
Version of due obeisance.
He seemed more than simply pleased
To see a Venetian youth
Do this without awkwardness
Or in a manner uncouth.
I had official business
With him—handing a Latin
Letter from an ambassador—
Which was written on vellum skin.
After my work as translator
Cum courier (with fulsome
Praise from Dara) had been tied
Up, he asked about the vellum:
'Not quite paper, not quite hide;
What is the substance so choice?'
I explained that European

Kings used this fine-grained device
For long-distance communion.

Attendant   [*Entering, very short of breath*

Sire, I've just this minute heard:
The vizier's dead! The bird
Flew off (don't hold me frolic)
After being hit by colic.

Busee   [*Crossing himself*

I never liked his role
But, well, God Bless His Soul!

Tavernier

I gave him gifts in too much haste
They must now all go to waste!

Manucci   [*Thoughtfully, almost as if in a
                               reverie*

So is Sadullah, then, dead?
He was never a friend of ours.
And I can hear it being said:
Lethal seeds of poppy flowers
(Or suchlike) were subtly mixed
In the good man's betelchew
Or, in his aperient, fixed
(The poor man was always 'due')
By none else than—Dara's faction.
'This deed's the work of Dara's men'
Will be one sure reaction,
*'Trying their damn'dest to stem
Aurangzeb's bid for power.'*

But how very off the mark
That would be! Rumours devour
Reputations like a shark
With an underside mouthslit
That smiles as it ingests
Honour's unblinking fleet
And then, nudging coral, rests.

Tavernier

I cannot say I am grief-
Struck at Sadullah's demise.
It's more a sense of disbelief
(Death sifts not, wise from unwise.)

Sadullah thrived through flattery.
He did, too, through intrigue.
He was the skilful votary
Of a faith that doesn't fatigue.
Faith, not in a just God
But in man's intelligence,
A faith to which I cannot
Subscribe without great reticence.

Cleverness is clever for a span
Alone. Unexpected Death can
Make the smart look quite sorry:
Placed, with brain baggage, in her lorry.

But having said this, I believe,
History won't be unkind
To Sadullah. He'll yet retrieve
An aroma from the rind
Of his life's desiccated
Story, partly because good

Persisted with the low-rated
In it, but also since he would
Be succeeded by men who are
Living gargoyles, not men.

Mir Jumla's not all that far
And plans to cross the Deccan's fen
To come, salute and—win the King.
He brings from Kollur's diamond mine,
A lustrous stone too large to ring
But, for crowns—anodyne!

Manucci

Clearly, Delhi is in pain.
She has been, before. But, alas,
There is a difference: To gain
Her Crown they'll now sell the lass!

ACT TWO

At Mir Jumla's camp on the outskirts of Delhi. He is on his way to the Imperial Capital to wait on Shah Jehan. And, later, in and around the Red Fort.

SCENE 1

The inside of Jumla's tent. Mir Jumla's coat of mail, sword and escutcheon are hung up on the tent's inner wall. A simple bed lies to one side. Jumla is seated on the carpeted floor. It is night. A lamp burns near him as he dictates letters to two secretaries who are standing on either side of him. Mir Jumla holds letters in the intervals between his fingers and—toes!

Jumla   [Addressing the amanuensis to
                          his right

Now take this down, with no mistake
    Soever: 'Exalted
Master, Prince Aurangzeb: I'll stake
    My well estimated
Career in arms and business
    On this undertaking.
Golconda was ours; its fortress
    Almost in our keeping
Until the so-called peace party
    At Delhi botched our plan

And snatched the urn of victory
 Waiting in the Deccan.
But with Bijapur, I promise,
 I will take no chances.
What melting hearts made us miss
 With self-righteous stances
Will now be 'ours'—I mean—'yours'.
 Get that right: *'Yours'* not *'ours'.*
And resume: *'Bijapur's forts*
 Will yield within hours
Of my besieging Kalyan.
 All I need is consent.
The Emperor of Hindostan
 May not, I feel, dissent
When we give him this reason:
 Bijapur's latest king
Is not his predecessor's son
 But a baseborn offspring.

'But what will finally click,
 Is not the "bastardy".
 I will daze the dove-clique,
And place it in true jeopardy
 By using another,
Much more irresistible,
 Ploy: of the jeweller!
"The South is a crucible
 Of gem-making sap,"
I'll tell him. "Its rich lava-flows
 Have formed the Deccan Trap
Where fluids metamorphose
 Into rocks and turn gems."
I will then show him evidence:
 Topaz petals, ruby stems

But above all, Great Heaven's
    Own gift to Kollur:
The radiating diamond
    Someone's termed "Kohi-i-nur".
That will be my last argument.
    Yours, most obediently,
    Mir Jumla,' Now transcribe
That fast. Neatly, evenly
And on it superscribe....

                    [A soldier enters, bowing

Yes? What's it that brings you here?
    I see you're not alone.
I thought I had made it clear
    That ... but you're just a drone.

                    [The soldier is at a loss to
                    understand his master's wishes.
                    Jumla dispels the doubt

Speak,
You leak.

Soldier

Most noble sire, I've been sent
With four prisoners who're meant
To be produced before you here
Since their crimes took place near....

                    [Jumla pulls out two papers from
                    between his toes and addresses
                    his amanuensis, ignoring the
                    soldier who remains standing

Jumla

Send these two letters to Delhi
And see they positively
Reach the Princess Roshanara
By morning. And see Prince Dara
Does not manage to get scent
Of them, else my fury I'll vent
On you and you and . . . well any rodent
Within sight of me that moment.

> *[The man takes both papers,*
> *bowing, while Jumla disengages*
> *another script from his left hand*

Now this other little note
That I, a while ago, wrote
Must be sent to my son
Through a rider other than
Him who takes the letter
To Aurganzeb. It had better
Be sealed by me directly
And confidentially.

> *[Affixes a seal himself and notices*
> *the soldier still standing*

I'll see your prisoners now.
Fetch the first and tell me how
He's in fetters. Did he plunder
Rape or commit murder?

Soldier   *[Bringing in the first prisoner*

This one entered a house
Slew a woman on some grouse

Together with three infants
And an explanation invents. . . .

Jumla

Chop his hands and feet,
And dunk him in some field
Near the main roadways,
To bleed away his days.

*[There is a moment of shocked
silence. Jumla illustrates his
intention with gestures*

Didn't you hear?
Get it clear:
Chop, hop,
Hop, chop.
Finger chips
In chilly dips!

*[The first prisoner, in a trance,
is pushed out and the second
brought in*

Soldier

This one stole on the high road
A pilgrim party's heavy load.

Jumla

Slit his stomach for seeking gain
Illicitly. Then fling him in a drain.
Gut in a gutter
Is better

Than brain in a drain.
Don't complain!

> *[The second solider exits, dazed,*
> *as two others are ushered in*

Soldier

These two are bandits plain,
They rob with complete disdain.

Jumla

Disengage their brainholders
From their flabby shoulders.

> *[The two are ejected from the*
> *tent. The soldier bows and leaves.*
> *Mir Jumla returns to his*
> *paperwork, extracting a folded*
> *note from between the toes of his*
> *left foot.*

Read out this closely-written note
From our office at Melkote.

First Amanuensis   *[Reads*

'My most noble chief
And lord of this fief. . . . '

Jumla

Cut out the salutation,
Come straight to the disputation.

'We have a strange case with us
Of a Rajput lineage
That is not just idolatrous
(It came here on pilgrimage)
But barbarously customed.
A weak-livered man of this host,
To our water unaccustomed
Sickened and gave up his ghost.
Now he was married to one
Who is no more than a child;
She is but twelve (I won
A bet on this), gentle, mild.
But on the day they burnt him, sire
They tried to force the poor girl
To mount the still-unlit pyre.
The little creature was in a whorl
Of terror, trembling, weeping
As she neared the spot.
Her agony as the leaping
Torch neared the fatal cot
Cannot be described in words.
Her kin had got her fastened tight
Lest she run away. I envy birds.
They pair but when the mate has died
Are free to just fly away.
We stopped the grim proceedings
In time. (The corpse was burned next day.)
The fair child to her in-laws clings
But they treat her as offal.
We have detained the lot of them
But on policy, we waffle.
We can be sure of one outcome

56

If they are freed: They'll abandon
Her. We need our Chief's orders
On this. Tell us if what we've done
Is right. Should within our borders
Customs beyond ours, prevail?
Should the South, the civilized South,
Not make such an attempt and fail?
Forgive us for raising this doubt.'

> *[The first amanuensis retires to*
> *one side. The second responds to*
> *his master's instruction*

Jumla

Take this down: *'I am amazed*
    By your doubt.
Whoever interfered was crazed,
    Or a tout.
He should be sacked at once.
    Your notion
That there is room, in governance,
    For emotion
Is wrong. It is also stupid.
    Don't waste time
On issues like this vapid
    Pantomime.
Customs are best left alone.
    A beehive
Congealed with honey may moan
    But just try
Intervening and you'll see
    For yourself.

If you want nectar, avoid the bee.
    Do not delve
Into the why and wherefore
    Of men's deeds.
Law is law, custom custom. Therefore,
    Their decrees
Cannot overlap. We uphold
    The former.
Leave convention to some bold
    Reformer
Of a future age. Do not dabble
    With men's mores
Or the manners of the rabble.
    It's their crores
Stashed away in stores that interests
    Aurangeb.
Release your wretched Rajput "guests".
    Don't be vague
On first principles. What becomes
    Of the wench
Isn't your business. Who succumbs
    To a wrench
Or matters of sentiment
    Is unfit
For a role in Government.'
    That is it.

Now take this down for headquarters.
    'In a letter
From one of our subalterns
    On a matter
With no importance to it
    He has confessed

That he gambled. *(Won a bet.)*
    I should've guessed
His nature earlier but never mind.
    He talks of birds.
Philosophises. We've been too kind
    To men of words.
Government can't afford thinkers.
    Have him transferred
As Jail Warden, where the clinkers
    Reek of turd.'

Soldier   *⌜soldier enters*

Most noble sire! I have the honour to report
Execution of the four orders of this court.

> *⌜Soldier and both amanuenses*
> *withdraw. Jumla rises, puts his*
> *remaining notes into a box and*
> *stretches his limbs, yawning.*

And now on to Delhi!
May it fill the belly
Of our great enterprise.
Not noble, perhaps, but so wise!

> *⌜He blows out a lamp, preparing*
> *to sleep. Jackal cries are heard*
> *as the stage lights dim and the*
> *curtain falls*

SCENE II

Two months later, in Shah Jehan's private apartments. It is very early in the morning. The emperor is ill and lives in bed behind a screen which conceals him from view. He has, at his side, Prince Dara, Princess Jahanara, Bernier, and a hakim. Jester stands by himself in a far corner.

Dara   *[Addressing his father near his bedside*

I know you're feeling wan
But, both doctors agree,
—It's now half-past three—
That you'll be better by dawn.

Jester   *[To himself, in a spot of light*

No! not by a half-chance
Though all his doctors dance.
He'll be ill awhile, I'm sure.
There won't be an easy cure.

Let me for the record
Proceed now to set out
The unfolding events
Of the next few moments.

The poor king struggles
And with Time, haggles
For a few more years.
But Time never hears
Pleas for an extension
Without suspicion.
*'Tell me what's so special
In you?'* An official

🌑 60 🌑

Speaking for Death, enquires.
Shah Jehan now perspires.

What should he volunteer
And what, never hear
Repeated? 'Well, I've been
A king.' *'Of kings I've seen
Plenty! Another,*
better reason, please.' 'Sir,
I've been a good monarch.'
He adds. 'Please see my work:
Forts, a mausoleum. . . . '
'O that! that's just Time's rheum.'

The man knows his Bible
And so chucks this pebble.
On the King's stained-glass painting
(Which comes, facedown, crashing:)
'What hast Ye done to Excess?'
Shah Jehan is in a mess.
His 'excesses' he dare
Not repeat. And from where,
In this bad disorder
Of his, can he order
A list of his good deeds?
But the official needs
It, if he is to speak
To Death. The case is weak.

But as often happens,
Someone else stirs and pens
A compassionate prayer
To the Lord and Master.
Princess Jahanara

And the Crown Prince, Dara,
Maintain that Shah Jehan
Is no vagabond khan.

He has established
The Rule of Law, banished
The Rule of the Jungle.
(They have a drafting bungle
There—Dara's a nature buff!)
But if that's not enough,
The son and daughter add,
Their good father has had
Just no end of trouble
From his three ignoble
Younger sons. No sooner
Then they've said 'younger',
Their prayer gets cut short
By this stinging retort:
'Younger sons? Now come, come
Was he not Prince Khurram
A younger son and prince,
Junior to Khusro, whence
Arose a contention
Between Prince Two and One
Which ended with Khurram
Enthroned, and "justice" mum?'

The man knows his History
And the family tree.
He will not change his views,
He says, and continues:

'Khusro was the eldest,
He was also the best.

But Khurram though younger
Proved himself stronger.
I know that Khusro died
(How, I will never find;
I was on leave that day,
A colleague bore him away)
Before Khurram was crowned
And the debate got drowned.
But next in line after
Khusro wasn't your pater
But Khusro's eldest son
Now, by choice, a Persian.
So I will buy no yarn
From dear old Shah Jehan
About seniority
And propriety.'

These thoughts of Death Office,
Cold and heartless, suffice
To strike son and daughter
As callous manslaughter.

Dara is distraught.
But Jahanara is not.
She loves him clearly,
Her father. Tenderly
She goes to where he lies.
Touched, he opens his eyes.
'By prayer time this dawn
Your illness will be gone,'
She whispers in his ears.
Is't an angel he hears?

If asked to summarise
What went before my eyes,
I'd say it went like this
(More or less, that is:
Shah Jehan was dying,
Dying very slowly.
Shah Jehan was lying,
Lying to history,
When a loving daughter's
Fervent prayer in verse
Made death change his orders
And recall the hearse.

*[The spotlight goes, the stage is
fully lit. It is now dawn and an
elated Bernier addresses Shah
Jehan.*

Bernier

I was, I confess, cynical
But your pulsebeat's turned rhythmical!
The heat has left your brow;
You will feel better now.

Jahanara

Allah the Merciful be praised,
Allah, the Compassionate!
To His glory let hands be raised
To Him, who determines our fate.

Dara   *[Going down on his knees. The
                        stage dims slightly, as a spot-
                        light covers him alone*

If I was being tested, Allah,
I know I've failed, my Bismillah.
I quailed before approaching death,
My faith puttered as Father's breath
Your Holy Name tried to suspire,
And I saw that what I aspire
Most is not his health or India's,
But *my* smooth climb to the dais.
In the prospect of Father dying
I saw my succession flying
Away like a Blue Rock Pigeon
Chased by the Shahin Falcon.
This peregrinator's hind claws
Struck primogeniture's soft laws
Mid-air, in one swift loop of power,
And took them to a crag to devour.
This vision, or one akin,
Princess Nadira had seen.
I had ridiculed her imagining
But now I saw myself fearing
Much the same thing. My thoughts wandered
From my father's bed and squandered
My bounty of faith in ambition's
Fickle bazaar. True contrition's
What is called for. I place it,
Allah, at Your Forgiving Feet.

Jahanara   [*The spotlight now shifts to her*
                              standing figure

I know that this illness began
With the dreaded Jumla's plan
Of inveigling the House of Timur
By his gift of the Koh-i-Nur.

The emperor was transfix't
By the luminous gift.
His pupils dilated large and gazed
At the fiery rhombus, dazed.
The phosphorescent stone osmosed
The optic rays and composed
A like response. The pair of eyes
And the stone then synchronized.
But diamonds are notorious
For flaws, or what various
Astrologers have termed *dosh*
(With which lapidarists don't close.)
These can afflict the owner
Most hurtfully and on a
Powerful owner spell
Disaster. Now who can tell
What *dosh* the Koh-i-Nur holds
But that it certainly bodes
Ill became clear to me soon
Enough. What seemed a boon
Was indeed a curse. The king
Has not been well since: something
That cannot be explained in terms
Of Doctor Bernier's 'germs'.
He is totally puzzled now
And within himself wonders how

The king has revived. He dare
Not admit it was prayer
That wrought the miracle.
He's science's Oracle!

*[The second call for prayer is
heard. Jahanara moves to a
corner of the room. All the men
gather at the opposite end.
Bernier withdraws from the room
as namaz is offered. When it is
over, all rise, Jahanara leaves
and Dara goes to his father*

Dara

I have not known you to pray from bed
And can well imagine how frustrated
You must feel. But it is entirely
In order for those unwell merely
To use their hands and pray that way alone.
Should that too not be doable, to just intone
The prayer. And failing even that, offer
To Him, in complete stillness, your faith's coffer.

*[Bernier returns and moves up
to Dara, touching him on the
shoulder. Dara and he proceed
to a side.*

Bernier

In my medical career
Of many a long year
I have not known a patient

Become quite insentient
And within hours recover
By the power of prayer.
My medical attendance
Was reduced to a redundance!

Dara

My good friend, can there is two views
On what's better: To have for doctors,
For the very best of them, no use
Or become their helpless prisoners?

Bernier

God forbid that anyone
Should be dependent on me.
But I do not want someone
—Not the King!—think me a zombie.

Jester   [*Whispering to Bernier
                                   mischievously*

By the way, Doctor Bernier,
Is it really hernia?

Bernier   [*Responding in embarrassment,
                                   under his breath*

O dear me, it is *not* hernia!
Its true nature I find unbecoming
To describe. Suffice it to say none here
Would have ever considered risking
His health for an aphrodisiac
Trip like the king had undertook
Against all advice, on a bivouac
Organized by some foul eunuch.

Jester *[To himself*

Alley on alley is sure to resound:
'For weak males Bernier a cure has found!'

[Jahanara returns and speaks to
Dara

Jahanara

I am told word is going round
That the king has died and the ground
Is being prepared to proclaim you
His successor. It seems a few
Have even converged at the fort's gate
And will be quite happy there to wait
Until they have heard and got
News of whether Dara is king or not.

SCENE III

A turret on the walls of the Red Fort, Delhi. A crowd, mostly poor, has gathered outside it. It is early morning. First and Second Heralds are talking to the people from their vantage point in the tower.

First Herald

Go home, don't waste your time,
There is no news.
Don't draw from me, in rhyme,
Some choice abuse.
Do you not have some shame?
Vultures flock thus
On hearing sickness' name.

Paanwala

Don't think it's the King's health
    That bothers us;
It's India's! Our wealth
    Makes you pompous,
Fat. It's *we* who have built
    This huge Red Fort.
And so we feel no guilt
    Of any sort
About assembling where
    We have a stake.
Therefore don't you dare
    Make that mistake.

Sabziwala

We have a stake,
Make no mistake!

Doodhwala

We built
This Fort;
No guilt
Of any sort!

Paanwala

I take pride in temerity
But also in brevity.
So what I have to say ought
To be both sharp and short.
It's we who pay the taxes
But *you're* the one who waxes.

All the nation's resources,
The imperial forces
Gobble. Why should we bear the strain
Of maintaining this huge drain?

[The crowd purrs in
appreciation. Paanwala is
encouraged to resume

If the prince takes a fancy
To some dandified pansy,
Or the king builds a mansion
For the object of his passion.
Why, if an officer of state
A wedding to celebrate
Needs funds, who provides it?
Who but us—the people—damn it!

We mayn't even mind a prodigal state
If at least in its bounds, we felt *safe*.
We can't go to Agra or Muttra.
Thanks to dakus, thugs etcetera.
And so if the king is seriously ill
Don't expect us to sit at home, still!
We feel we're entitled to find out
Which of the princes is in, which out,
If Dara, the eloquent waverer,
With Jahanara (and those who favour her)
Will sieze power or will become
A Khusro plastered by Khurram.

Sabziwala

The man has wit,
Let us grant it!

Second Herald   [*Incensed, he shouts at all of
                                         them*

Just go, I tell you, *git*!
        Filthy vermin!
Are any of you fit
        To determine
The state of India's health?
        Has even one
Of you used *your* own wealth,
        Or a distance run
For someone else's sake?
        No, you have not!
So don't you talk of 'stake'
        And suchlike rot.

First Herald   [*To Paanwala*

Tell me, sitting here, just this:
        Have you given
Away, free, one single *paan*?
        A good haven
You've found to vend your ware.
        'India' today
Is your business, not care,
        You roll, I pay!

                                    [*Addressing all the crowd*

The king's ill. But what's new in
        Being unwell?
He is also human!
        Have you been well
All your lives? And when not,
        Would you like it

If all your children got
        Together to sit
And speculate your demise
        Or your last Will?
You would, I surmise, feel
        Yet more ill.

Thelawala

He speaks both wisely and well;
The paanwala's wily as hell.

Mochi   [*To Thelawala*

I know the herald's a good man;
        He always leaves a tip.
He once an obstacle race ran,
        Which caused his shoe to rip.
(The cleavage was where the upper
        The undersurface meets.)
'Keep this extra for your supper,'
        He says, 'Get yourself some eats.'
Then he takes my hand
        And says, 'You know you've played a role
You'll never understand.'
        'What?' I ask. 'You've just Saved My Sole.'

                    [*There is some excitement from
                    behind where the heralds stand.
                    Dara appears*

First Herald

Hail, Prince Dara Shukoh,
Crown Prince Dara Shukoh!

Dara

Friends, you have been waiting long
    For some news, I know.
The news I have, I won't prolong;
    Its brief, like life, but so ...

Thelawala

Life is brief, he said
The news must be bad.
His face looks quite red,
Anxious and sad.

Dara   *[Continues*

  ... So nuanced as to need explaining
    Too. But for the news, first.
The king *was* ill, complaining
    Of fever, aches and thirst.

Sabziwala

'Was,' he said. So he must be better.
The king must have recovered later.

Dara   *[Resumes*

The French doctor Bernier
    Tried western medicine.
He is very sincere
    And fights illness to win.

But medicament works not
    If faith is frayed—
A truth I had forgot,
    But my sister prayed. . . .

A Voice

Which sister,
Boil or blister?

Another Voice

One's a stunt
The other a.....

> [*Dara tauts with rage. But
> restrains himself as well as the
> two heralds who want to jump
> into the crowd to teach it a lesson*

Dara

For some months now I have been studying
    With a Jesuit priest
Holy scripture and its scripts.
    It has been a treat
To hear him on the use, abuse
    Of words, both wrong and meet.
I've often thought about swear words,
    Urban and bucolic.
I think these go with culture,
    In naukar or in malik.
Someone here, I see, employs
    His own brand: Pure Phallic

I can only pity the man
    Who fouls his mouth with these.
His abusive tongue's gone fungoid:
    It rots the word it speaks.
The profanities just heard
    Are thick, viscid grease.

I am not renowned for a cool head
　　　But I'll stay calm today.
My morning namaz I can yet hear,
　　　So I'll keep anger at bay.
The toxin jabbed into me just now—
　　　I'll stop in a tourniquet.

I will not let my bloodstream carry
　　　Poison to the brain today.
Anger and like passions can perhaps
　　　Be permitted play
On days of normal circumstance.
　　　But today, Fate holds sway.

All of you, I am quite sure, believe
　　　That life's a journey
In which you have a destination
　　　And, perhaps, the money.
But getting there depends not just on
　　　You, but on Destiny!

Almost everyone of you has
　　　A daughter to wed
A complex spouse to take care of,
　　　A parent in sickbed.
Sometimes all these situations
　　　Land at once on your head.

And some of you may be afflicted
　　　With other tensions
Too: a crazed sister, hare-lipped son
　　　Showing predilictions
Of the most unbecoming kind.
　　　These are enervations.

Stretch the scene and you have: debts unpaid,
    A pathan you must dodge;
And because of lingering blood feuds,
    A complaint you must lodge
Which, in turn, involves waiting on
    Some bureaucratic podge.

[Dara pauses

Sabziwala

He sure understand us,
    Dara does.

Dara

One person who understood people
    And their humanity
Was our Holy Prophet Mohammed.
    He brought equality
Between rich and poor, weak and strong.
    Brought solidarity

Through means of a common prayer
    That went beyond kinship.
Unions of family and tribe
    Cannot confine worship.
Everyone was free to come and pray,
    Child, cobbler and Lordship.

Doodhwala

It's as if he's been to our homes
Not just stayed amid power's domes.

Dara

But alongside these demands of life
    Which drain your energy,
You have another, exacting goal
    That admits no lethargy.
A goal that calls for nothing less than
    The purest synergy.

Paanwala   [*Barracking Dara again*

What be *that*
Cat or rat?

Dara

If I have used a strange-sounding word,
    It's strange only in sound.
Its sense—harnessing man's will to God's,
    Powering square with round—
To each of you is self-evident.
    The poor can be profound.

                    [*There is a murmur of*
                    appreciation as Dara continues

Each of you has talent but also
    More, though you don't know it:
An ability to turn matter
    Into the purest spirit.
Else how does a benighted weaver
    Make fabric that's sunlit?

How does a yokel's wife transform,
    With a half-broken quill
The walls of her rude tabernacle
    Into an epic 'Still'?

It is because she has a margin
      That has transcended skill.

Paanwala

The only margin we know of
Is one that you would scoff. . . .

Dara   [*Addressing Paanwala*

Let *me* interrupt you for a change.
      I well know *your* margin;
The profit margin you seek to widen
      To your glee, our chagrin,
By camouflaging unworthier leaves
      In a slick of resin.

                              [*Paanwala rises to protest but
                              changes his mind and sits down
                              again.*

Thelawala

You can say that again.
What won't he do for gain!

Mochi   [*To Thelawala*

From just one look at men's feet
      I can spot a cheat.
It's not that theirs are dirtier
      (Dirt's not my métier)
But theirs are larger and splayed
      With toegaps displayed.
And yet in slim shoes compressed,
      Like perversion repressed,

Cheats would like their feet, outsized,
    To reside, disguised.
For pairs of feet, there's nomenclature
    That goes by their nature.
Paanwala's I'd say, are classical
    'Perfect Rascal'.

Blind Beggar

Don't stop, Prince Dara,
Ignore Paanwala.

                              ⌈Together

Ignore him,
Ignore him.

Dara   *⌈Pleased with the clear shift in
public opinion*

Every one of you has this margin,
    You can take it from me:
An unknown, great dimension.
    Consider our friend, Dhunki.

                    *⌈Dhunki has been sitting
unnoticed all this while. He gets
a start at the mention of his
name*

He doesn't just fluff up our quilts,
    He also thrums a ditty!

Why? Who told him to? Did you, did I?
    Take Bhishti sitting there.

                    *⌈Now it is Bhishti's turn to be
startled*

His goatskin-bag's a mystic symbol, not
  Just a water-carrier.
The slain beast says, 'I'll slake your thirst
  Though you didn't heed my prayer.'

Or take that miserable wretch
  Who sits alone, yonder.

[Nur, a madwoman sits at a far
end, oblivious

People call her mad, and so she is,
  But for reasons beyond her!
Her crow's foot eyes were lovely once till
  A young man duped her.

He promised marriage but, post-facto.
  Nur obliged, 'What matters?'
Sure enough, he evaporated, and
  She rued, 'Life shatters.'
When a baby came to her, unwed, her image
  (And brain) went tatters.

But how many of you know this
  'Mad' Nur can fortune read
Not by the criss-cross on your palm
  As much as from rapeseed?
She'll make you choose one from a heap and
  Unerringly, proceed.

Blind Beggar   *[For all to hear*

I know that. She'd warned me decades ago,
That I'll be blind before I'm forty
Unless—*I fed my pet cat more!*
I laughed, and saying 'Don't be dotty,'

Chucked the seeds (and made her grumble).
Today, when I'm as blind as a bat,
Coming this way I hear Nur mumble:
'That comes of being unkind to a cat.'

*[There is general laughter. Only
Paanwala remains unimpressed,
unamused*

Dara

Why am I saying all this to you?
    Some of you may wonder.
Heralds may even start worrying
    What pressure is Dara under?
Why does he speak of Dhunki, Bhishti
    And Paanwala, sunder?

Is there some method to his madness
    Or is it unalloyed?
Dara's not mad by any means but—
    His taste for pelf has cloyed.
With me Panoply sits ill at ease.
    She's happier, viceroyed.

Some Voices

Dara Shukoh, Zindabad
Murad, Shuja, Murdabad!

Dara

Let us not wish Death to anyone.
    That's base.
All of us have God's breath in us,
    In any case.

We live and have our being
     With His Grace.

You know I have been made Crown Prince,
     Shah-i-Buland-Iqbal.
My mother wanted all this for me,
     The late Mumtaz Mahal:
A golden seat beside Father's throne
     And honours at Durbar.

It is not that I don't value these.
     I do, most gratefully.
I won't shirk responsibility.
     But I won't use a pulley
To wheel, raise or hoist myself to power.
     And I won't be a bully.

> *[There is applause, Paanwala*
> *alone demurring*

Paanwala

Oh yeah,
Dara?

Thelawala

We know you won't.
Don't heed his taunt.

Dara

I feel my true place is not in mansions
     But in a hermitage
Where those like Great Sarmad,
     And many a blessed sage

83

Practise rigour of mind and body
    And God's dominion, presage.

My place is also here, with you,
    Somewhere in these mewses.
For if this spot is one where our
    Paanwala abuses,
It is also a place where, surely,
    Some new Rumi muses.

I for one have always held
    That on these very cobbles,
Right amidst our day's companions
    Some unknown Surdas hobbles.
Tell me, don't you rate his songs higher
    Than palace baubles?

Blind Beggar

God will bless you, Dara,
And the Begum Nadira!

Dara

I have often contemplated
    Priests engowned in surplice.
Yet wouldn't you say ill-clothed Kabir just
    Routs those in God's office?
He sure tempts *me* to bid all Power a
    Polite 'khuda hafiz'.

I wish I had no compulsions:
    A father's loving hope,
Brothers who though ambitious,
    With India cannot cope,

The court's several functionaries
　　Who in ignorance, grope.

I spoke just now of India
　　And also made a mention
Of ignorance. By the first I meant
　　No physical nation
But the fact that India is a—
　　Civilization.

Blind Beggar

Yes, a civilization,
Not just a nation.

Dara　　　　　　　　　　　　*[Warming to the response*

India is a sanctuary for
　　The world's earliest faiths
When they are banished or distorted
　　By corporeal wraiths.
But more, India gives protection
　　As our sage sayeth,
To the faith underlying all faiths:
　　That Man is half-divine,
Is meant to complete the process
　　And his base self, refine
By giving up strife, envy, deceit,
　　Notions of 'mine' and 'thine'.

India is not meant to be a theatre
　　For belligerence.
Not meant to be witness
　　To a dance of ignorance.
And yet—those in charge of her—
　　Prefer intemperance

85

Of every kind! I am no prig.
But those who are in power
Have been given a sacred trust
Though for a brief hour.
They just cannot come to treat it
As their in-law's dower.

My office, palace, golden seat,
Parallel *your* day's woes,
Your chores, your cares, your debts, your feuds
With near and distant foes.
My jurisdiction represents
The tough soil a peasant hoes.

Just as all of you balance
Your duties to your folk
With a duty to your own *within*,
Your Self, with your Daily Soak,
So do I too equilibrate
My yearnings with my yoke.

Paanwala

A yoke?
What a joke!

Dara   *[Taking no notice of his heckler*

I know that as a prince I need
To custom conform.
I know that as Crown Prince I should
Certain duties perform.
But most of all I know I *must*
Some practices reform.

Thelawala

Yes, Dara, please perform,
    Please reform!

Dara

Of these the first pertains to when
    The Emperor is ill.
Princes are prone to view that time as
    A vacuum they can fill.
Instead of praying for his health
    They start to scour his Will.

Sabziwala and Doodhwala

Shame,
Shame!

Dara

Worse, they start to forge his 'Will'
    As also alliances.
They read the khutba in their names
    And taking no chances
Quietly ensure that their force
    To Delhi, advances.

Now, last night, when Father lay ill
    My mind was filled with fear:
Will this dread sequence re-enact
    In high or low gear?
This thought disturbed me so much,
    I forgot my prayer.

Though I forgot to say my prayer
    Yet Allah intervened.

After the longest night I've known
    Or so to me it seemed,
Father recovered—a miracle—
    And the doctor beamed.

I come to tell you this today,
    But not this alone.
I also mean to tell you that
    Dara can atone.
Atone for forgetting Allah
    Who yet has mercy shown.

Thelawala

No more atonement is needed
When the prayer's been heeded.
That should your dilemma resolve,
And guilt, if any, dissolve.

Dara

Those are sage words, so simply said,
    Simple words, sagely expressed.
Before returning to Father's side
    I would like this stressed
Whenever it is time for me
    I *can* climb the crest.

Blind Beggar

You must, Dara, you must,
You must climb the crest!

Dara

Yet I will do *with* all of you,
    As your friend, not ruler.

When I, if called upon, *your* throne ascend,
        No one will be my broker
Save all of you, my people,
        And—our common Maker.

Thelawala

I'll be with you always
On bylanes, roads or highways.

Mochi

I'll make the slippers
For your coronation.
They'll have silken uppers,
Subtle decoration.

Blind Beggar

Don't forget to invite me
Dara! Be sure to sight me.

Subziwala

Hail Prince Dara,
Crown Prince Dara!

                    [*Dara salaams and leaves. He
                    does not hear Paanwala's parting
                    shot*

Paanwala

Don't think this halleluiah will crown you.
Murdered Sadullah will drown you.

                    [*Thee is commotion, with the
                    crowd pouncing on Paanwala
                    who yells in pain*

First Herald [To second Herald

I am afraid, it's started already
The beginning of the end, so bloody.

Second Herald

The wicked are provoking the good;
While the good are quite unwise.
Agitation has never stood
Athletes well; they drop the prize.

ACT THREE

Two weeks later, at Dara's mansion, Shahjehanabad.

SCENE I

Father Busee and Dara are in conversation in Dara's private room. Both are seated on chairs. It is morning.

Dara

I've longed for a pastoral lease,
    Holding a shepherd's crook
Watching soft, slow-moving fleece,
    Beside a gurgling brook.

Busee

The shepherd's crook,
Its slender hook,
Are symbols
That help assemble
Men's thoughts which stray,
To the pews to pray.

[Jester bounds in, breathless

Jester

Sulaiman Shukoh. Sends a message:
    Shuja's doings presage

 91

War. Shuja's proclaimed: *'The King is dead.'*
  Murdered by you, he's said.
His father's 'slaying' he will avenge.
  Will take his own revenge.
He's sending forces. Will climb the throne.
  He calls you a trombone.
Only fit, he says, to blow a trumpet.
  (Also, slave of a strumpet.)
No one, Shuja says, can try convince
  Him the King lives, no prince
Anyway. He heads towards Agra
  And dares you, Prince Dara,
To stop him. Should his revered parent
  Still live, 'Heir Apparent'
Says he will, in joy, his two feet kiss.
  But on you, he'll jet a . . .

Dara   [*Rising in a delirium of anger*

Shuja, you malignant tumour,
  Cyst of rumour,
Suppurating abscess
  In pig's recess!
You ingrown, grime-lined toenail,
  You lizard-tail,
I'll excise you with triple slicers,
  Dice with my incisors.
Don't you dare, just beware. . . .

Busee   [*Touching his elbow*

Prince, noble prince, forbear.
  It's not easy
Under such an unfair
  And sleazy

Attack, to maintain calm
　　Yet try this balm:

[Crossing himself

You must indeed wield a knife,
　　But steadily.
A surgeon's shake can end life,
　　Unwittingly.
Please go to your father,
　　Take his counsel,
Staying cool rather
　　Than thermal.

Christ once swept rogues,
　　And money-changers
Out of a synagogue's
　　Foyer. Scavengers
Must be resolute, not angry.
　　Ignore dog-snaps,
Look confident, not hungry
　　For the street's scraps.

Dara　　　　　　　　*[Regaining his composure
　　　　　　　　　　somewhat*

Shuja's been known for indolence.
　　What's new is insolence.
Let him be a voluptuary,
　　Ours is a free country!
But let him not for a moment presume
　　He can assume
Power through disinformation,
　　Character assassination.

I know I shouldn't have lost my temper
    (Anger's such a tempter!)
But when I heard that wicked bit
    About 'slave of strumpet'
My composure's little ampoule burst
    And my slanderer I curst.

Even now, when I think . . .
—Jester, get me a drink—
Of Shuja as he busies,
My sight blurs, my mind dizzies . . .

                    [Dara rushes out even before
                    Jester can fetch water

SCENE II

In Shah Jehan's apartment. He lies, bolstered by huge cushions on a couch. Dara and Jahanara stand beside him. Sulaiman Shukoh stands to a side.

Dara

I have now seen the entire text.
    Shuja's dropped his mask.
Whatever it is that he does next
    I think I know my task.
What he's trying to do does not behove
    A scion of Timur.
Shuja must be made an example of,
    An example that'll endure.

    Though you have been unwell,
He knows that you are much better now

And yet at Rajmahal
Crowns himself, assembling a force somehow
    Crosses into Bihar.
And ravaging villages down the route,
    Shows his hand from afar:
'Delhi I'll sieze and on the way, I'll loot.'

An army must be sent at once
    To combat Shuja
He must not be permitted
    To cross the Ganga.
He must be turned straight back
    From Darbhanga.

Shah Jehan   *[Speaking with difficulty*

Let Shuja's advance be stayed
    And by . . .
(Please do not be dismayed)
    One I
Love, trust and can command
    To go,
My grandson Sulaiman
    Shukoh.

Dara   *[Somewhat take aback*

You've made me proud—and worried!
    My son is brave.
He's always been ready to
    Jump into the fray.
Yet this is sudden. My father,
    Just one thing I'll crave.

Let Sulaiman command a force
    That is strong in men

—Some twenty-two thousand at least—
    With boats to cross the fen
And Jaipur's Raja Jai Singh to serve
    As his wise guardian.

Shah Jehan

All this, please take as done.
    Now godspeed,
My beloved grandson!
    Mind your meed.

Sulaiman

I will leave at once,
    Leave at once, I will;
I give a fond grandson's
    Word: This rising I will still.

> *[Sulaiman bows deeply before
> Shah Jehan and Dara who
> embraces him. Father and son
> leave the room together,
> accompanied by Jahanara. Shah
> Jehan is alone and soliloquizes*

Shah Jehan

I must say I like
    His mettle.
And yet, Allah, *I'm*
    In a nettle!

Parenthood's strange:
    Shuja has rebelled.

And I can easily gauge
    He must be expelled
From this town, that village.
    But ought he to be *felled*?

No, I will tell good Jai Singh,
    Go flay
Shuja's small uprising,
    Don't slay
The poor, dopey princeling!
    I must not delay.

> *[Claps to call attendants,*
> *who rush in. The curtain falls as*
> *Shah Jehan begins to give them*
> *instructions*

SCENE III

Some days later, in Dara's apartment. Dara, who is in high spirits, and Nadira, are talking. She stands while he is seated at his floor desk. Jester stands, typically, leaning against a wall.

Dara

It has been a signal win,
    A great victory.
Our valiant son has saved
    India's glory.
He and Raja Jai Singh have made
    History.

At the head of mail–clad horsemen
    Brave Sulaiman

Surprised Shuja's unvigilant troops
    Which then ran
For dear life, is grapeshot disarray,
    Blasting Shuja's plan.

Mirza Raja Jai Singh's help
    And guidance
Have meant a great deal,
    Have done immense
Good to our cause. He is endowed
    With a sixth sense.

He deserves a *saat-hazari*,
    I'll tell the king.
A robe, a mansion in Delhi,
    Or some such thing
That will vouchsafe his family's
    And his well-being.

Nadira

I am not a Rajput princess,
Who only wants her son to *win*.
I have a mother's heart within,
Which seeks his good, nothing else.

For me, a son gone to battle,
'Midst flutt'ring pennants, glinting swords,
Is still the babe in swaddling clothes
Clenching his tiny rattle.

I hope he won't take long to come.
His young wife and children are here,
Deeply wracked by nervous fear
Though she wears a smile and seems calm.

Babur's sons have now fought enough.
Please give yourself a chance to live.
Forget pride and greed, forgive.
Tread the smooth road, give up the rough.

Jester

Your lady speaks most wisely.
　　　But who wants wisdom?
Good sense, too, is miserly
　　　In this mad fiefdom.

> *[Nadira prepares to retire. Jester
> urges her to stay*

If the Begum does not mind
　　　I've something hard to say—
To both of you: Please be resigned
　　　To going either way:
Success and a joyous return
　　　For good Prince Sulaiman
Or—failure and a rude turn
　　　Of events. That man
Jai Singh's no sage counsellor.
　　　He let Shuja escape.
While your son, a clear victor
　　　Stood shocked and agape.

> *[Dara tries to question Jester
> but he continues regardless*

I have it on good authority:
　　　The prince was quite matchless
In courage, tactic, celerity,
　　　But the Raja, callous—

On purpose! Sulaiman's prize
    Reached him, to be snatched.
But before he could organize
    Chase, a small plot was hatched.
Prince, your new Seven Thousand
    Wallah is treachery
Incarnate. His perfidy'll land
    Your cause on slippery
Slopes, just you mind! He had been asked
    —Was he not?—to see to't
What Sulaiman was tasked
    To do, worked? He's done the opposite.

                              [Sipihr Shukoh darts in

Sipihr

Our bhishti is just back from court.
    Watering the grass
Outside the Diwan-i-Khas
    He heard a report.
It's frightening, Abbajan.
    Crossing the river at
Akbarpur they now aim Dharmat,
    The hordes from the Deccan.
And, Abbajan, Gujrat's forces
    Under Uncle Murad
Have teamed up, and stand guard
    With the Deccan's horses.

                       [Dara rises, tensing, like a newly
                       stretched bow

Dara

Am I Crown Prince or a slave
    That news of this import
Should reach me via a bhishti
    Rather than from the Court?
Intrigue lines every nook and
    Corner of the Red Fort.

Jester   *[To himself, in a spotlight*

Now opens the Tale of Treason
    When princes' greed,
Beyond all reason,
    Outstripping need,
Will turn brothers into butchers,
    Some into gnomes,
Make them produce savage ruptures
    Within their own homes.

Dara   *[The spotlight shifts to Dara*

I do not quite know
    What this is, though.
A challenge to be crushed
    With troops rushed
Or a stupid little attempt
    Meriting mere contempt.

I cannot believe that Jai Singh
    Has betrayed the cause,
Has let Shuja take wing,
    Quiet loyalty's laws.
Or could it be that his gambit
    Was cleared *here*?

Was he *asked* to transit
    Shuja, for fear
Of Sulaiman's righteous wrath?
    I will never know.
And now on Narmada's froth
    Comes he deadlier foe.

Aurangzeb and Murad combined
—Sharp brain upheld by brawn—
Are more than we had bargained
    For. Shuja has flown,
While the younger two have junctioned.
    So if Delhi hasn't lost
Yet, it has not quite functioned
    Either. I must
Now enter the proceedings
    Myself, not trust
The court to handle these things.

SCENE IV

*Shah Jehan's apartments in Red Fort. He is now able to sit
on a large throne-like chair. Dara and Jahanara occupy
smaller seats.*

Shah Jehan

Ganged up, have they, those two?
    The sly brats.
Too scared, singly, to face you.
    Sewage rats!

Let Dharmat be their doom,
    Can't they see

I'm alive, my court's in bloom,
    Prosperity
Rules the land? Let your mailed fist
    Smite their faces
Give their heads so tight a twist
    Their act collapses.

Let Karim Khan and Jaswant Singh
    Be your generals.
Let their vim and valour bring
    The minerals
Of a successful expedition
    To our smeltery
For a final separation
    Of gold from emery.

Dara

Father I must beseech you to bestow
    All I may need to power
The State's war machine. I cannot go
    Into battle and cower. . . .

Shah Jehan   *[Interrupts Dara by clapping his*
                               hands for attention. Some half a
                               dozen men, including officials,
                               enter

Let every courtier,
    Officer of State,
As may chance to be here
    Hear me ordinate:
Prince Dara's *mansab* is increased
    By ten thousand *sowar*
Ten thousand *zat*; through *his* decrees
    Speaks *my* power.

I leave for Agra tomorrow,
    To convalesce.
Dara's words my thoughts borrow;
    The two coalesce.
He will now be your Sovereign
    In any affair,
Whether internal or foreign,
    Everywhere.
Heed him and him alone,
    Turn to no other.
After I, to Agra, have gone
    Dara is your ruler.

[The courtiers bow and with-
draw. Dara rises and follows
them. Shah Jehan talks to
Jahanara

Shah Jehan

I love him most dearly
But also fear for him.
His nature is pearly
White, but with a sharp rim!

As for the other three
—the world's well aware—
Shuja's just too carefree,
Murad not quite 'there'.

While the third, Aurangzeb
Is, in exact balance,
At once wily and brave.
The two spell competence.

And also disaster
For all his relatives
(Excepting one sister)
Who seem alternatives.

I wish he was not brave
And wily, half and half,
But brave three-quarters, knave
One quarter. On behalf
Of wiliness, I'll say
A State needs cleverness.
One like Tavernier
Could have saved us this mess.

Yet, Aurangzeb's kind of cunning
Leaves me cold and wondering
If my kingship and parentage
Will collapse, a moral wreckage.

Dara is not wily,
He is God's warrior.
But with zero savvy
Still, a foe-harrier.

Dara is impetuous,
Fighting for good causes,
But most tempestuous,
A fire-spewing Moses.

I want him to be King.
For he's a noble son.
But I can't help worrying
He's not the ablest one.

Just see my child, this fate.
I have a large estate

To leave behind to sons.
Should I choose the sharper ones
Or him who is good?
The answer wears a hood.

Jahanara

I know you are for Dara,
Why then this palaver?
Aurangzeb's my brother
Too, but you know him, Father.

Shah Jehan

I'll put it this way.
I want Dara to win.
Want goodness to hold sway,
Nadira to be Queen.

And let me be quite frank:
Aurangzeb is a freak
(I sometimes wish he drank!)
The other two, too weak.

But, and there is a but,
I have a paranoia:
If the war at Dharmat
Kills my beloved Dara
And leaves the other two
Crippled or crazed for life,
Who'll rule India, who?
The sole survivor's *wife*?

Jahanara

You can never be sure
Who'll die, who will endure

In this or that battle.
But one thing I'll foretell:
If Aurangzeb succeeds
At Dharmat, he proceeds
To Delhi. Not to 'kiss
Your feet' but establish
Himself as Emperor,
Father, your successor
Even when you're alive!
And the Court will connive
With him in this. If only
You gave Dara free scope, Delhi
Would be safeguarded. But
He's restricted; he's undercut.

Shah Jehan   *[With some irritation*

Ifs and buts don't make kings;
Kings make ifs and buts.
It's their right to shape things
By promptitude and guts.

I know my duty clear:
Both Kasim and Jaswant
Will be told to adhere
To this line: 'Recalcitrant
Princes need a lesson.
Give it loud and clear.
Yet protect their person
From gun and rapier.'

As for Dara he must
Stay here. He must rule
In my stead and should trust
My judgment; not be a fool.

SCENE V

The Diwan-i-Khas. Dara is seated on a smaller throne beside Shah Jehan's which is empty. Attendance in court is poor. An officer wearing a tilak on his forehead stands near him, depressed.

Dara   *[Wringing his hands*

I should have gone myself,
    Directly faced the brunt.
But deferring to the King
    Lapsed my own judgment.
This error will not repeat;
    I'll now be a combatant.

Flesh out the fiasco for me:
    Who held the Narmada,
Who crowned what eminence
    To halt the invader.
Did they, to hold one river,
    Want a whole armada?

Officer

Most noble prince, being summer, the river
    Was fordable and the enemy
On the other bank, fatigued and in fever.
    In fact just a part of its army
Had come up. If we had only crossed the ravine,
    Victory would have been in our hand.
Some officers in their artillery opine
    They were unprepared to fight and
Feared we would cut them off from the water.
    But we did not cross the bank to fight.

Had we done so, the resultant encounter
    Would have ended on our side that night.

We gave the enemy a gift of three days' rest
    After which it opened cannon fire
And moved forward under that cover to wrest
    Its victory. Most noble sire,
Raja Jaswant Singh showed exceptional mettle,
    Disputing every single inch of ground.
Eight thousand Rajputs were with him in this battle.
    Almost all of them were slain in that round.
Kasim Khan turned traitor; he gave no support.
    His crucial division let us down.
The Khan fled the field, leaving Jaswant to report
    Defeat and turn towards his hometown.

Dara

Has Kasim Khan shown up somewhere?
    Has he opened his mouth?
He cannot hope to run away,
    That miserable lout.
I must get an explanation
    For his strange performance.
Was it fear—an abomination
    In soldiers—or worse—malevolence?

Officer

The defeat and carnage were the direct result
    Of advice Delhi gave Kasim Khan.
He was told to adopt the Jai Singh gestalt.
    There was a clear, though secret, ban
On taking the battle to conclusions which might
    Injure, much less kill, the two princes.

This restraining order for Kasim Khan sufficed.
     He obeyed with the 'right' devices.
But Jaswant Singh on being sounded, straight refused.
     Like seed unto a vedic firepit,
Jaswant and his valiant Rajputs were used.
     As the fire climbed, the skies were lit.
Full golden grains of Rajput sire and son
     Chanting 'Har, Har' plunged in, turned carbon.
And all this while, Kasim Khan's men stayed back, tight.
     The ladle pours, but itself stays safe.
Prince, Kasim Khan's men fed the fire's huge appetite.
     He's home at Agra; Jaswant's a waif.

Dara

Someone tells me Jaswant's proud queen
     Their fortress doors has barred.
To him for having survived defeat.
     A Rajput, battle-scarred.
If vanquished, sands disgraced for life.
     Jaswant has learnt that, hard.

But his valour will be rewarded.
     Homeless wanderers
Are preferred in Heaven's judging eyes
     To power-panderers
Or to Delhi's fast growing tribe
     Of trust-squanderers.

But, to turn now, to where action lies.
     I will now to Agra vault,
And give battle, a battle I will win.
     No one dare Dara halt.
Dara will smite and dispatch his foes
     Like a thunderbolt.

The King's mind is now distracted,
    A passive canister
For others' thoughts, both good and treacherous.
    I see one minister
Urging that diplomatic messages
    Go to Prince Sinister.

I see another pleading with
    Princess Jahanara:
'*Please suture wounds,*' then going straight to
    Rouse Roshanara:
'*Now's the time, the ideal time, to cut*
    Poet-Prince Dara.'

War-mongers will propose peace, as
    Peace-makers opt for war.
I will be called a belligerent,
    A man who thirsts for gore.
They'll say I cry for fraternal blood
    While they '*just knocked at our door*'.
The King, I know, still hopes against hope
    To turn the princes back,
He thinks they can be reasoned with,
    Saved from getting the sack.
He does not see the invaders' game
    Will make India crack.

Rao Chhatrasal and brave Rustam Khan
    Will not to the Chambal go.
The two will hold in strength the line;
    They will humble the foe
Even before I have got there,
    Or Sulaiman Shukoh.

Sulaiman's army hastens here
    To help curb this rebellion.
A son, a father and grandfather
    Will together rely on
Cosmic justice to teach the rebels
    Their life's biggest lesson.

ACT FOUR

Aurangzeb's camp in the woods of Mandu, three days later.

SCENE I

The Viceroy of the Deccan sits at a plain desk in an austere tent. An informer from Delhi who stands near him has just told Aurangzeb of Dara's faith in cosmic justice.

Aurangzeb

Remove the 's' from cosmic,
And you will Dara mimic.
Dara is a pygmy,
A dwarf, if you ask me.

> If I had been eldest
> Yet not, alas, the best
> I would have left power
> For a hermit's bower.

Would have let abler men
Do what's beyond *my* ken.
Would not have turned jealous
And let War befall us.

> The other two have merit,
> You cannot deny it.
> Shuja as a viceroy
> Holds Bengal like a toy.

Murad, as another,
Keeps Gujrat in tether.
As for me, I'm a mere
God-trusting *fakir*.

I have no ambition,
No false sense of mission.
I would rather sew caps
Than pore over war maps.

Much rather calligraph
Bind folios in soft calf.
I would not disappoint
Adze or nib-point.

But in this quatrain,
From self-praise I'll refrain.
(My vaunted self-restraint
Is real, not a feint!)

My life-style is subdued
I'm not the one to feud:
I am a man of prayer,
Of His will, an obeyer.

I covet seclusion,
Dislike all profusion.
Not for me music, dance
Rhapsody or romance.

I cannot speculate
As Dara can, or meditate.
I am, as I've told him.
Just a simple Muslim.

Yet Dara calls me names.
Says I am playing games.
Calls me a *namazi*
And Shuja a *hafizy*.

What, may I ask, is *he*?
A fluttering pansy.
A pansy in a crown!
That man is but a clown.

Tell me, *can* Hindostan
Be left to such a man?
Dara's a good wordling,
He is not meant to be King.

I'll leave word-formulae
To him. I am a lay
Believer who is pious
And minds his own business.

But will *he* leave statecraft
For his true field: wordcraft?
Of course Dara will not;
A 'teacher' can't be taught!

If the King were not ill
I might have remained still.
But now the die is cast,
The suspense cannot last.

I have told Prince Murad
'You're too big for Gujarat;
Timur's throne awaits you.
You have skill and sinew.

'After the war's over
(The King can't recover)
You—Murad—will be crowned
While I stay Deccan-bound.

'Meanwhile I go to war,
For you in Dholpore.
I'll seal off the Chambal
And see his ego tumble!'

SCENE II

A week later, at the Diwan-i-Am at the Fort, Agra. Shah Jehan has had a setback and is standing with difficulty. His arms rest on Dara's shoulders. The hall is full of ministers, courtiers, attendants. Bernier and Manucci are also present.

Shah Jehan

I feel like some ancient grandsire,
     A *Mahabharat* man
—I can't get his name—Mother didn't tire
     Of repeating it.
Was it Bhishm, Dhritrashtr, I forget.
     The fact is I am ill.

And deep inside me a hollow gong
     —Tabla struck in the eye—
Goes *dhung, dhung, mridhung*! What's gone wrong?
     What? Nerves, head, heart? I don't know.
My blood congeals, bones sag. I get
     The warning my pulse beat strays.

I send my beloved son to battle
     With whom? Two others sons.
A grandson just returns, whose prattle
     My ears remember.
From where? From another engagement.
     With another son.

As recently as one week ago
     I thought this would avert.
In Delhi I still felt like King, but oh,
     Now I feel like dying.

116

You rightly counsel restraint.
    I am old and infirm.

My well-beloved and cherished son!
    I hoped to see you king
Peacefully, without battles lost or won.
    But who can fathom Allah?
I had also hoped to go forth against
    The two unworthies myself.

I have just one advice to give:
    Prolong the proceedings
Till Sulaiman returns, so you can weave
    A net of warp and weft
In which to trap those two rascals
    Unfit to be brothers.
Trap them son, but . . . those two are uncles
    To your boys, remember.

I won't see one son slay another,
    Uncle behead nephew.
I would rather that your mother
    Had smothered them at birth. . . .
What am I saying? I am sorry, son.
    I know I am rambling.

I can see that I now forfeit
    My right of converse.
Forgive me, Dara. Forgive my bleat.
    But that's what I've become:
A goat transvestised into a lamb,
    A lamb for the slaughter.

I bid you, Dara, Win This War!
    Not so I can stay King;

So I can stay *sane* and the State, inure,
    Take one hundred thousand horse
Twenty thousand foot
    Eighty legs of cannon.

Dara

Father, as from today,
I am a combatant.
Soldiers are not to say
That they have sentiment.

I proceed to Dholpore
For to win this battle
I will trace the spoor
Of this snake-with-rattle.

I will surely get him,
Slinking in his outlet.
I will then de-fang him,
His venom I'll goblet.

And all this I will do
Quite emotionlessly
For passion can undo
The future of Delhi.

I'm a man of feelings,
Very strong attachments,
But hearts need low ceilings
In soldiers' cantonments.

This I do assure you,
I go as Timurs go:
Not just for victory,
But to make history.

Our lives are a river
That flows from source to sea.
Most see it and shiver
But some others, get busy.

Father, give me blessing,
Your soldier-son needs it.
But send me no Jai Singh
Close on heels, to mess it!

SCENE III

A corridor in the The Fort, Agra. Jester stands alone, against a wall

Jester

That was Dara, classic.
Using words like plastic.
But I know he forced them.
For form, he composed them.

Composed them in croc-skin
Cold, scaly, plasticine.
How can the heart reside,
In protocol's dead hide?

Take his bit on the river
And how most men shiver.
I know what he'd have wished
To say, but hubris dished:

'Our lives are a river
That flows from source to sea.
Some try dam its vigour,
Others just let it be.

I'm not sure who is right:
The ones who opt for peace
Or those who go with might
To wall up its soft crease.'

That is what Dara feels.
When free, not when he kneels
And tries form to appease.
His choice? The soft crease!

I'm going to the war
I am not staying back.
I've never been before

> [*Dara enters, Jester does not notice*

In a soldier's shack.
I want experience
Of the actual thing
And perhaps my clairvoyance
Could help our future king.

Dara

Ho, pipsqueak! And, as always,
I, my, I! Look, you just can't

> [*Jester gets a start*

Come to the front. And who says
Armies need a clairvoyant?

But you won't listen. So all right,
    Then, come along.
But just stay out of sight
    When the fight's on.

Shah Jehan's apartment. He peers through a balcony. The
dome of the Taj can be seen framed by it. Jahanara is beside
him.

Shah Jehan

There he goes, my noble son.
    In a cloud of dust.
May he come back after he's won,
    Like a tusker in musth
But I fear he won't return.

             [Jahanara looks at her father,
             anguished

    At least, not victorious.
You know of Nur the Taciturn—
    The one in Delhi's mews?—
While viewing one of the Taj's designs
    Once, I heard Nur mutter
'Who builds mansions for the dead, consigns
    His sons to the gutter.'

Jahanara

As opposed to that, there is this
    Rain of blessings
Prayers, charms, hosannas,
    Love's outpourings,
Which have been showered on Dara
    By folk with feelings.
Simple folk with simple leanings.
And he carries with him the
    Benediction

Of that great Comforter of Souls
    (My addiction)
Khwaja Muinuddin Chishti.

SCENE V

Roshanara's parlour in the Fort, Agra. The princess is talking to a female attendant.

Roshanara

Ask the eunuch to ride post-haste,
    Overtake the retinue
And reach Aurangzeb this message:
    'Dara plans to dupe you
With a seeming halt-and-wait
    By his assorted crew
Manning Manucci's cannons.

'But his real intention's to
    Send one flying column
Under a dashing officer
    —Chhattrasal or Rustam—
To watch your movements right along
    The Chambal variorum.
And thus prevent your crossing.

'So you must ford the river
    East of where Dara's headed.
It's lucky the stream is subtle
    And complex its bed.
Dara also brings new matchlocks
    With (it is said)
Greater speed of delivery.

'But the most important message
Is: we are fortunate
Khalilullah Khan himself
Paid me a visit.
Before he left with Dara.
I'll be brief: *he'll do it.*
He is Jai Singh and Kasim incarnate.'

SCENE VI

Aurangzeb's tent at camp. It is night, past ten. He is reading softly, reverently, from the Holy Qur'an by lamplight. During a pause, a rustle is heard. Aurangzeb continues. It is heard again. He pauses from his reading.

Aurangzeb

What is it this rustle, this vibration,
This unwelcome insinuation?

[Turning towards his right

Ah, a snake outside its radius!
Scaly, cold and hideous.
It calls for a quick transition
From Arrival to Excision.

*[Aurangzeb draws a little sword
and with one swing separates the
reptile's head from its body. He
claps. Attendants rush in and
are aghast. Aurangzeb does not
speak but with gestures asks them
to clear the mess. He then resumes
his reading. When it is over, he
stops. A messenger enters*

Messenger

Most Noble Prince, we have learnt
Of your swift dispatch of the serpent
That strayed into this honoured tent.
More than a snake, to its end, has been sent.
A message has gone; we've seen an Omen!
Aurangzeb will be King! Amen.

Only he can rule India, who stays calm.
India's safe in Aurangzeb's palm.

Aurangzeb

My sword is *His* dagger
I've no right to swagger.

Messenger

Our good princess Roshanara
Has sent me as a signaller.
Knowing its contents I'll prefer,
If you permit me to whisper.

> *[Whispers into his ears
> Roshanara's information.
> Aurangzeb responds after a
> minute*

Aurangzeb

Bless you, Roshanara
For this sweet cantata.
I was getting distrait
About my future fate.
Reports had come to me
About the enemy.

'Dara's is a pageant,
A great war regiment:
Tuskers from Anuradh
Stallions from Baghdad.
Cannons and musketry,
Masses of cavalry.'

One of my brave Baluch
Quoted the gunner Manooch:
'We move like an ocean
In tremulous motion.
Dara 'mid his squadron,
Resplendent like the Sun.

'Shines, a crystal tower
That brightens by the hour.
Around him ride Rajput
Of the highest repute.
Their tall lances sparkle,
Their red glances crackle.

'Dara's own elephant
Is just magnificent!
Tusks with gold-encrusted
Blades which can't be rusted.
That pachyderm, Fath Jang,
Itself is rippling young.'

All this made me wonder
If I hadn't made a blunder
Pitting my resources
Against Agra's forces.
I began to miss Jumla,
And his battle éclat.

Miss him most keenly.
And with hourly
News of war imminent
I turned hesitant
To pit my small war-skills
'Gainst Delhi's power mills.

> But, denied Mir Jumla
> I've now got Khalilullah!
> He will be at Dara's end,
> My unsuspected agent!
> Nothing can be better
> In war than an abetter.

SCENE VII

Samugarh. May 1658. Dara's war-shack. It is situated on a promontory, commanding a view of the battle. Swords and helmets lie about. Jester is its sole occupant. He is watching the proceedings from the shack's opening. The sound of cannon fire is heard intermittently.

Jester

It's started a little too soon,
Sulaiman is not yet here.
Dara should've waited till noon.
Sulaiman is so very near!

> Dara's a prisoner today.
> Prisoner of his destiny
> Will it, or will it not permit
> The mystic to match the 'hermit'.

Dara's exposed himself to death.
He would just not listen.
Rustam said 'Look they're on the heath,
We're above—a safe position.

'Logic and practice tell us:
Be still, like a gecko; don't fuss.
Reserve your final part
Till you can up and dart.'

Sage counsel can sound dull.
More so when cunning's at large.
Spoke Khalilullah: 'Don't mull
Over tactics; just charge.'

Now, nothing spurs Dara as much
As a hint that he has lost touch.
'To the attack!' he thundered,
Poor Rustam just surrendered.

Time, I'm sure, will bear me out,
Khalilullah's a treach'rous rogue.
No single act can bring a rout
To Dara as this prologue.

Rustam's back in his division
(Khalil is in levitation!)
Dara's now mounted Fath Jang.
'Jai, jai!' proclaims every tongue.

But in the pit of my stomach
I have this feeling: Dara's sunk.
For I can see Khalil slink back,
And *he* had said 'Don't funk!'

Dara smiles in self-confidence.
He signals his men: 'Come, sons
Join me in this victory!'
Orders drums to sound history.

I notice the foe does not stir.
He waits for Dara to near,
Precisely what Rustam said's wise.
Rustam gave such good advice.

[Cannonfire is heard

There! the enemy has fired:
Cannons and dread musketry.
Men and tuskers both get mired.
And shaken is our cavalry.

But Dara smiles again! He waves:
'Continue the advance!' Rustam raves.
His men fall. Yet with Chhattrasal
He groups and rushes to Dara's call.

Now what's Dara trying?
Like rolled-back seawaves
He spirals and—comes lashing!
Great God, the foe caves!

He has rammed into the enemy's face—
Through darting arrow and flying mace.
They lie prostrate, stupefied,
Some, from shame, their face hide.

Dara's broken through their guns
Ripped their camp, put it to rout.
See, see how that fellow runs!
Without doubt, he's won this bout.

Some of his brave soldiers—Daud
And Firuz Mewati—have proved
That if your cause is just,
Your enemy will bite the dust.

> Missiles hiss out in greed
> Prince Dara to receive.
> His shield's got filigreed,
> His morion's a sieve.

Is it courage or conviction
Or just a mental affliction?
The man's mad, in one sense,
Madness can twin innocence.

> Aurangzeb's 'touched' as well.
> Unmindful of Dara's challenge
> He asks for his ranks to swell,
> To try return the lunge.

But Khalilullah, it is plain,
Has no desire to be slain.
He has stayed off the engagement.
He won't, with Luck, experiment.

> Brave Chhattrasal and Rustam
> Tear through enemy barriers
> Such is bravery's custom.
> They are its noble carriers.

I can see Dara greeting them.
'Well done!' he is telling them.
They put his hand to their breasts
As for one moment, Dara rests.

Dara looks composed and ready
For another joust with death.
Lord! this tournament is already
Out of breath.

As Dara's mahout pricks the tusker,
He misses an arrow by a whisker.
This battle has no ground logic.
It proceeds by sheer magic.

They charge again and again
The Rajputs shout '*mar, mar*!'
A speared horse screams in pain.
'*Khuda Hai*'! comes from afar.

'*Khuda Hai*!' Aurangzeb bellows.
His steed bursts a varicose.
He now mounts a tusker: 'Forward!'
But it stands rooted, trunk lowered.

Dara's the clear victor,
A clear victor is he!
His brother will be taken,
Taken he surely will be.

But wait ... Dara pauses. He bends.
Listens to news someone sends.
Looks shaken, turns, touches his chest.
Lord! What is this sudden test?

*[A herald rushes into the
warshack*

Herald

Even as our prince was winning,
Traitors in our ranks were plotting

130

Dreadful murder. It is said.
Chhattrasal and Rustam are dead.
Shot by arrows from *our* side.
Now where will loyalty hide?

> *[He leaves and Jester resumes
> his observation*

Jester

If Dara breaks now, it's over.
But ... he erupts! His elephant
And he are a ball of fire!
They singe the enemy's front.

> They hurtle to its left flank.
> Which at once goes blank.
> They turn now towards the right
> To take on Murad's dread might.

Murad too is elephant-borne.
His howdah's now a porcupine:
Arrows its four sides adorn.
Murad gives and takes rapine.

> Elephant faces elephant:
> This deadly, that defiant.
> Brother faces brother;
> Both hiss at the other.

They are far, I can't see faces.
But I think as Dara raises
His spear, Murad grimaces.
Does he say: 'My eyesight glazes.

'Is that Dara who embraces?'
Dara can melt in love's mazes.
But of course, I am dreaming.
Dara's spear tip is gleaming!

But what's this now? Khalilullah!
Whispering to Dara? Dara's quiet.
Hey! He dismounts! Allah!
The howdah's empty. There's a . . . riot!

'Where is Dara? Dara's gone!'
His soldiers cry forlorn.
The mahout helps clear the doubt
'There he is!' But now it's a rout.

Anarchy has taken over.
No one listens, no one cares
The traitors are in clover.
And how well rumour fares!

When Murad is all but finished
Gullible Dara's vanished!
Why did he leave the elephant?
His enemy is triumphant!

Dara's men wail, 'He's killed!'
They scatter in confusion.
Dara sees he has been diddled;
Regrouping's now out of question.

Through my tears I see him ask
'Where is that bloody a . . . ?'
Where *but*? Dara asks too late.
Khalilullah's well past the gate.

With Five Thousand Horse (his strength)
He's gone over—he's bolted—

To Aurangzeb; he's done the length.
He's jumped, pole-vaulted!

> Not *one* of his men got a scratch,
> Not one! Rustam is a red patch,
> Chhattrasal, fallen dead.
> On both the fleeing forces tread.

Dara runs from someone crying
For water to another
Reduced to a stump, dying
With a soundless moan, 'Mother!'

> Dara darts from slain horse to soldier.
> He touches one, shakes the other.
> And over corpses, leaping,
> He finds young Sipihr weeping.

Sipihr was in command himself,
I'd seen him brave, confident
Till his division rushed to help
His father, when it all *went*!

> Samugarh will mark a turn,
> From which Dara will not return.
> Why did it have to end thus?
> Busee! Cut your cant on Jesus!

Acharj! Drop your drip on dharma!
Dara was on goodness' side.
He had impeccable *karma*.
Dara's been taken for a ride.

> His men and faith lie slain here.
> Tell me, Lord, that art Supreme
> Wilt thou help Dara clear
> The debris of his dream?

SCENE VIII

Three kos from Samugarh, on the route to Agra, stands a shady tree. Dara arrives under its canopy with some half a dozen attendants. They have dismounted, earlier, from their horses.

Dara

> *[Taking off his helmet and sitting down beneath the tree*

Is this for what Hind
Has been destined?

> *[Distant kettledrums of victory, sounded by the Aurangzeb- Murad forces are heard. Sipihr lies down beside Dara, placing his head on his father's lap*

Sipihr

I can't understand this.
Abbajan, I can't stand this.

Dara

Nor, son, can I.
An evil eye,
Perhaps,
Traps
Us.

> *[The boy closes his eyes. Dara strokes his head*

Traps
Us, perhaps . . .
A very evil eye.
Neither you, son, nor I
Can understand
This, or stand
Here . . .
Sipihr . . .
Sipihr sleeps
And in his slumber, weeps.
His grandfather paces forlorn
Between empty hall and a vacant throne.
Is it true, Dara, that you've been routed?
Your victory had not been doubted!
The King wanders
And ponders
The reason:
Treason.

SCENE IX

Dara's apartment at the Fort, Agra. It is nearly midnight.
Dara has just about managed to return from Samugarh with
his personal guards. He leans on a table, talking to Nadira.

I can't bring myself to face the King.
I don't know how I fell in the ring.

How can I tell him I was betrayed.
By a trick Aurangzeb played.

He will say, rightly too, a soldier
Ought to be an integer.

Ought to be able to play a role
That's not split up but whole.

I should not have been just audacious
But sly and suspicious.

For every soldier deployed
A spy too I should have employed.

For every volley of cannon fired,
I should have had a rumour sired.

In the fabled *Mahabharat* war,
Truth lied to switch the score.

'*Ashvattham is dead*!' the message went
When Bhim slew the namesake elephant.

'Ashvattham, the warrior, was prized.
Great Dron the father stood, paralysed.

Dron had arched his bow when guile
Neutered the projectile.

If the righteous Pandav could lie
Why should mundane Dara not try?

In war, manners are not a good creed.
You must sow division's seed.

Lies punctuate war's grammar;
They put truth in inverted commas.

Perfidy is the steaming kiln of tricks
That provides War Monument its bricks.

Father, with pain etched on his brow,
Will rail at me for my poor knowhow:

'You were meant to snatch your victory,
Not go down in Failure's history.

'Snatch it by leaning where quick wit leans,
Not bothering over ends and means.

'Gone is my dream, gone your enterprise.
Gone your 'ilahi; shattered, hope lies.'

I will not know what response to make.
No explanation his thirst can slake.

'Khalilullahs will manipulate
Don't decry them, rather, emulate!

'He asked you to quit the howdah
Ostensibly to dodge gunpowder.

'His true aim was, of course, different
In wanting you off the elephant.

'A howdah without an occupant
Like a necklace without its pendant,

'Turns all individual heroes
Into just as many zeros.

'You're seated now, strong, brave, Titanic,
And now, gone! There is instant panic!

'He did his duty as per his lights.
Did you have to go by Jesus Christ's?'

Father will twit me with questions.
Fling at me countless aspersions.

I cannot and will not so submit
To probings which don't God admit.

I go now, princess mine, not vowing
Triumph—that's pride—but, still, unbowing.

Unbowing to strength and stealth alike.
I have no compromises to strike.

I will leave before dawn has broken,
Will go before the thrush has spoken.

There is no time for me to squander.
I will, for quite some time now, wander.

My flight will not be for Delhi's throne
But for avenging Rustam's moan.

I will avenge the brave Chhattrasal
Who has joined his head to the *Harmal*.

My fight will not be just blood-for-blood,
That's orthodox. *I will be a flood.*

I will treason's fortress inundate.
Honour my slaughtered soldiers' mandate.

Nadira

I am going with you.
I know nothing of blood,
—And do not see any flood—
But I'm going with you.

Dara

You are hardly strong enough!
My home will be a wild course.
My plate, my palm; my glass the trough
I'll be sharing with my horse.
Princess Jahanara will
Take care of you and Sipihr,
Till Sulaiman returns. Still. . . .
If you are bent, so be it.

ACT FIVE

The routes along which Dara moves, with Nadira, and a progressively diminishing force.

SCENE I

The Red Fort, Delhi. Dara is in the Diwan-i-Khas which is empty, except for Sipihr Shukoh, Jester and about three or four officers. Nadira sits in the ladies' alcove. First Herald enters and addresses Dara who is seated on his smaller throne.

First Herald

My Lord, Agra suffers collapse.
Prince Aurangzeb now has the Fort
And our King is in prolapse.
This is the distressing report.

Dara   *[Stung by the news, he stands up*

O, that I should be here
    In Delhi's safety
When Father, you're a prisoner
    Of Fate's cruelty.
I will yet play a role, Father,
    I'll defy this travesty.
I know for sure that Aurangzeb
    (That snake 'mid vermicelli!)

To proclaim himself Badshah
    Will now turn to Delhi.
But he won't find me here
    Though search he every alley.

SCENE II

That night at a rear gate of the Red Fort, Dara talks to First Herald.

Dara

Good Herald, take this message
    To Prince Sulaiman Shukoh:
I fly to Punjab, with his mother,
    Prince Sipihr and retinue.
He must join me there very quickly
    And let Prince Shuja go.

First Herald

I curse fate that I should say farewell
    Thus, to my noble lord.
But worse has overtaken Second Herald:
    He fell to the enemy's sword
At Agra Fort three black nights ago
    While fighting the horde.

The good seem to be dying out,
    While the bad go to town.
Yet lord, surely, it cannot be that
    Destiny's a let-down.
If you do not succeed, my prince,
    In the Jumna I'll drown.

But consider this: You and Prince Shuja
    In league in the East;

Punjab and Kabul unsubdued, Golconda
    Without its beast
(Jumla will move north), Jaswant Singh
    Angry, to say the least.

This, with Prince Murad's disenchantment
    And Prince Sulaiman beckoned,
Still constitute a formidable force
    Prince Aurangzeb's not reckoned.
The cause is not hopeless, though we cannot
    Rest; not for one single second.

Dara

I thank you truly for your thought,
The sweeter for being unsought.

SCENE III

A spot on the eastern bank of the river Beas. It is evening.
Dara, Sipihr, Jester, Daud Khan and three soldiers are seated.
Nadira is reclining, propped up by Sipihr.

Dara

I'd hoped Shuja would rise in Bihar,
    Jaswant in Rajasthan,
So Aurangzeb can get off our trail
    And we save Hindostan.

Daud Khan

The Prince yields too quickly to despair
The Qur'an holds despair infidel.
There's time yet our future to repair
And break treason's foul citadel.

SCENE IV

Multan. Dara speaks to soldiers who want to desert him.

Dara

Are you fighters or freebooters?
    Have you no loyalty?
Soldiers who flee from their armies
    Must face a penalty:
A loss, for all time to come, of
    Their credibility.

A Soldier

That word's too big for me,
    My good Prince.
But I get the message.
    Eloquence
Is not needed to put me
    In my place.

You are entitled, Prince, to scold us,
    You have suffered.
And we are grateful to you for all
    You've offered.
You've been kinder than many who are
    More coffered.

But a soldier only speaks soldier;
    I'll be plain.
In battle, we'll face most dreaded risks
    With disdain.
But Prince! We can't for ever follow your
    Luckless train.

SCENE V

Dara's reduced camp on the right bank of the river Indus.
Daud Khan and Jester stand beside him.

Dara

So Murad, you said, is now taken prisoner,
    The poor sodden fool!
By flattery beguiled, by temptations inveigled.
    'Not I, Murad will rule,'
Protested Aurangzeb: the 'hermit', Aurangzeb,
    'I'm just his vestibule.'

Aurangzeb has used him, ambition has seduced him.
    By a metastasis,
Where Murad would have sat, Aurangzeb is seated.
    The two brothers' axis
Proceeds unerringly now to our
    Dynasty's catharsis.

Jester   *[To himself, in a spotlight*

Murad's in the cooler,
Aurangzeb's ruler.
Shuja on the run,
Heightens Aurangzeb's fun.
And as for Dara
—Our solfatara—
His occupation
Now is air emission.

SCENE VI

Sirohi, near Ajmer. In a small, shack-like tent, Dara is dictating a letter slowly to Jester, addressed to the ruler of Mewar, the senior Rajput prince.

Dara

Begin by saying, 'Hail, Maharana Raj Singh,
You are, verily, the Sun of the Hindu race.
I recall, with great pleasure, our last meeting
When, thanks to the late vizier, you had to face
Impending ruin. It was my great privilege
To intercede in the case and see justice done.
Your Highness is aware that our King and liege
Has been held captive after the usurpation
Of his throne. Hundreds upon hundreds of Rajputs
Pathans, Hindus and Muslims have been slaughtered
By the upstart prince who, now in Delhi, bruits
Unqualified triumph. Some of us are quartered
In your territories. We entrust our honour
To your keeping and come as guests of Rajasthan.
You're head of this vast tract, I am in a corner.
I seek your help and that of the whole Rajput clan
To liberate our great King, restore his throne.
My specific plea is for Two Thousand Horse
With which to help the King, harkening to his groan.
I trust on you alone; I have no other source.'

Jester

What about the family matter?
It's lost in political chatter.

Dara

Add this as a postscript:
'My wife is indisposed.
I might be, thus, adrift
For days: she must repose.
Can your gracious Ajmer
Be home away from home
For her, showing the care
I cannot, since I roam?'

SCENE VII

Two days later, at the same venue. A rather stiff messenger of
the Maharana is standing near Dara. Daud and Jester stand
a little apart.

Messenger

His Royal Highness, the Maharana
Sri Raj Singhji, Pride of Rajputana,
Has commanded me to convey regards
To Prince Dara. The Maharana guards,
He says, the fortunes of a mighty race
By being its protective carapace.
Joining Prince Dara in his enterprise
Could his whole community, jeopardize.

[He leaves with a nominal bow

Dara

A new principle I now propound;
As Dara's law to be renowned:
Mistrust The Person You Rescue,
He Will Be The First to Ditch You.

145

SCENE VIII

The following week, March 14, 1659, at Deorai, just south of Ajmer. Jester, as at Samugarh, is in Dara's war shack. A battle is on between Dara's rudimentary force and Aurangzeb's army. Jester records its progress.

Jester

Aurangzeb has chased him
To Mewar's outer rim.
Dara is on the mat
For yet another combat.

> Shunned by every Rajput,
> Dara's tried like Canute
> To wish war-waves away.
> They return, anyway.

But this one wave he'll fight,
Dispute his brother's might.
Dara stands on one hill
To baulk Aurangzeb's will.

> Flushed with his victories
> Over 'refractories',
> Aurangzeb also stands
> Upon a prominence.

Dara's soldiers, though few,
Are nonetheless of his hue:
Audacious, brave and bold,
They dare Aurangzeb's hold.

> Ahmedabad's Shah Nawaz
> Able, gregarious
> Has joined Dara with guns,
> Large, crackling cannons.

But Dara's out-martialled,
He's out-generalled.
Aurangzeb's massed forces
Can mark Dara's solstice.

Brother sees his brother,
Sons of the same mother,
At his own antiphon,
One shrill, one baritone.

They stand silhouetted,
Each to each rivetted.
Who'll fire the first shot,
The tension will unclot.

[A cannon is fired

There, it goes with a boom!
Dara's won elbowroom.
His horsemen now descend
On Aurangzeb's hill end.

Sulaiman's erstwhile 'guide'
Is at Aurangzeb's side:
Mirza Raja Jai Singh—
That wound without dressing.

His sight ignites Dara:
'You bastard let-downer!
Killer of my son's pride
I'll rip your turncoat hide.'

But Dara this time round
Wishes to be more sound
In the style of his fight.
He will stay out of sight.

He monitors each move
From a cautious remove.
But this can lower, snarl,
His men's battle morale.

But what's that commotion?
A whole hill's in motion.
Dara's men rush forward—
To be overpowered.

They've zoomed into a spot
Where Shah Nawaz, I thought,
Was in command.
But Death is a gourmand.

It's picked brave Shah Nawaz,
Shattered the top brass
Of Dara's small army.
It has sided the enemy.

'Fire!' Dara bellows.
'Jai Singh an answer owes,
To Sulaiman Shukoh,
And Nawaz, now no more.'

Plonk! They shoot. *Plonk, plonk, plonk.*
Dara wonders 'What is wrong?'
There's silence in the ranks.
The guns have fired blanks.

'*Bl . . . blanks*? But how, why?'
'Don't talk,' they say, 'just fly.'
Aurangzeb's forces climb.
They've won an ally: Time.

It's getting to be night.
Dara's in the twilight.
The Sun, red, luminous
Lends Dara a nimbus.

But against the fire-disc
Dara runs a risk.
He's seen, as he tenses,
Through Aurangzeb's lenses.

'For God's sake, run,' he's told
'You'd be silly, not bold
If you just stand and wait
To meet Nawaz's fate.'

Dara knows its over.
Deorai. Samugarh.
Sipihr and good Daud
. Point at deserters, queued.

'We're not superhuman,'
They say. 'We've got children.
Some risks we'll surely take
But suicide's a mistake.'

At Samugarh traitors,
Here infiltrators,
Have dashed Dara's chances.
Aurangzeb now advances.

Dara has been taken,
In his trust mistaken.
His highly trained gunmen
Had, in their ranks, villains.

Too easily suborned
These trust-betrayers pawned
Their office and their ranks,
Switched cannonballs with blanks.

They now cheer, wildly;
Aurangzeb smiles, mildly.
'Wasn't that *too* easy?'
Jai Singh nods. (He's wheezy.)

I am just putting words
To faces and gestures
But cannot be far wrong:
Dara's sold for a song.

He leans on a large rock,
In a state of shock
Not known to him before.
'Were they *duds*? Are you sure?'

SCENE IX

Disappointed and betrayed in Rajasthan, Dara lurches further east. Nadira is grievously ill. Bernier chances upon the benighted caravan on a highway. He examines her and reports to Dara, somewhere along the route.

Bernier

Time runs out for her now, I fear.
Her end, with each breath, draws near.
She has will-power, in plenty,
But even that's a futility
In circumstances like the present,
Prince, a mishap I can't now prevent.

Dara

I have this satisfaction, good friend,
That towards this very bitter end
The ailment was studied by your eyes.
I know you are frank, you are wise.
Know, also, that Fate is merciless;
It is shredding me with a cutlass.
There is, for Nadira, no hope.
But why was it silent, her horoscope?

Bernier

I do not know of a sorrier
Tale of swindling than Deorai.

Dara

After the 'rout by duds', worse followed.
Infiltrators did not spare my stores.
My wagons with treasure had billowed.
These were plundered, left with but their doors.
Protectors turned marauders; guards, thieves,
Having looted their fill, they scampered.
Nadira said, 'I have your album's leaves,
They're with me; can never be tampered:
A treasure no one can take from us.'
That placed a poultice on my great ache.
I saw that man's truest possession's
Love and its small tokens; the rest's fake.

SCENE X

Dara's rump now staggers towards Gujarat. The party is waylaid by a robber, Kanhoji.

Kanhoji   [*Brandishing a sword, challenges*
                                           Dara who rests on a large rock

Halt! Quietly pass up all you've got;
Koli robbers for compliance, wait not.

Dara   [*Smiling, after an initial shock*

A robber, are you? At least you're honest!
Clean robbery such as yours, is best.
I've been robbed already, robbed spotless clean.
My caravan yonder, too, has been.

Kanhoji

I saw it parked there, saw it silent;
Wondered what its quiet meant.
But tell me first, who or what you are.
You are unusual. I see, by far.
A nobleman fallen on bad days.
A prince, perhaps, repelled by the world's ways?

Dara

Why, you are no robber, but fortunist!
As for me, you're right, I've been through a twist.

Kanhoji

You aren't Prince Dara by any chance,
Are you? His news precedes his advance.

Dara

If indeed, I were he,
What would your reaction be?

Kanhoji

I would tell him, robbers can be gentlemen
And 'gentlemen', robbers; a court's no heaven.
I would tell him, now a refugee,
'Fear not. I *will* pilot thee'.

Dara

Dara, I am, my noble friend,
Pilot me to this desert's end.

SCENE XI

Kanhoji escorts Dara and his small party to Cutch, from where Dara crosses over to the borders of Afghanistan, seeking both refuge and allies. He camps near Dadar, Malik Jiwan Khan's fief, with Nadira who is now sinking, Sipihr, Jester and a few faithfuls. A vaidya and hakim are attending on her. Dara is in his tent with Jester.

Dara

If only Manucci had been there,
No gunman would have dared betray
His office or dare insinuate
Blanks into our side to create. . . .

[*A soldier enters, quaking*

Soldier

My lord, my prince, forgive me; I wish I had fallen dead
At Samugarh or Deorai, bathed in battle red

Than that I should be chosen to give this news: She is
    gone
Our noble princess, India's queen-to-be is now gone.

[Dara freezes as Jester breaks into sobs

Dara   *[Forcing each word out*

I was dreading this moment; I had seen it coming, though.
    Closer by the minute, a many-bladed dart.
It has got me now; cut me into a hundred bits.
    Each too stunned to fall, too weak to stay apart.
I have to take but one step and I will break into shards:
    Husband, prince; lover, soldier; one part head, one
    heart.

I would that you did not stand there where you do, to
    speak thus.
    But you do. I see your news is very real.
Cold and hard as the mail you wear; curved and sharp as
    the sword
    You bear. I wish you had the power to heal
The wound you have caused on my heart, my soul, my
    whole being.
    Fortune has orphaned me. Now this, my fate does
    seal.

[The vaidyas and hakim enter, hesitantly

Come, gentle physicians. I have the news. She is gone.
    My Nadira is gone to her rest. Gone from this mad
    world.
You did your utmost, you both did, as did Bernier,
    earlier.
    But she was past potions, herbs. Her flag she had
    furled.

What could have saved her, tell me, when the Fates are
    against me?
    She's dead, Nadira is. Into her grave, she's curled.

And yet I never thought she could die. I thought her
    deathless.
    But then which thought of mine has ever proved
    true?
Damned fool, Dara! Damned fool to have thought Nadira
    could
    Survive so many draughts of my life's bitter brew.
My life's been that of a stag hounded by sharp-toothed
    cheetahs
    Up creeks, down ravines, deserts and forests, through.

Zigzagging through thorns and thickets, across oceans of
    sand,
    Was I not mad, tell me, to bring with me my doe?
Luckless fate has dug its fang on her ere it bears me
    down;
    Dug its fang and sucks away her life so . . .
'Sucks?' I have my tenses wrong, I see. It's over, know.
    I see your thoughts, good vaid. 'He's unhinged, poor
    fellow.'

But, of course! I should be, even if I am not. Unhinged
    From a throne, from home, from friends, why, from
    Luck!
I was thought unhinged at the best of times. In court,
    wily
    Sadullah said as much of me. Now *he* had pluck.
Unhinged, he said. He's mental, not just temperamental.
    He covered my reputation with unhinged muck.

But wait, do I dwell too much on myself? I do, always.
    'Your thoughts beguile you, my prince,' Nadira said,
    too.
'Your thoughts are like peacocks. They come, preen,
    unfurl their plumes
    And dazzle you.' So they do, I owned, so they do.
'But then they immobilize you, make you their prisoner,'
    She protested. This took place at Fatehpur.

It was evening, the zephyr was abroad. Her garment
    billowed,
    Her earrings tinkled. I said to her: 'Princess mine,
My would-be queen, if my thoughts, you say, like a
    peacock prance
    Be my mate, and with me dance tonight, princess
    mine;
Let us to the riverbed go, a Moghul belle and beau;
    Let us dance by the Jamna tonight, princess mine!'

She held as her true ideal, the noble Khadijah
    Our Holy Prophet's faithful and loving wife
Who gave the Prophet support during his despondency
    And when, as Ibn Ishaq tells us, his meed was strife.
Khadijah was God's instrument to comfort the Prophet
    When he faced the scorn of men as, indeed, of life.

                      [Jester breaks down

Well you might sob, Jester; you more than others. She's
    gone.
    It's you who conveyed her from city to camp,
Then from camp to camp, camp to hideout to hideout,
    Under the fire-pouring sun (fools call it 'Heaven's
    Lamp'),
Which maddened our frothing horses, gladdened our
    gabled foes.

It's you who helped her on disappointment's steep
ramp.

Jester, yesterday, with two other horsemen rode off
    Saying, 'I'll get a hakim.' He knows my thinking
And so added, 'A baid as well; somehow I will get them.'
    Three dust-trails rose in their tracks, not to my
    liking.
They formed themselves into three gnome-like shapes:
    Shuja, Murad
    And Aurangzeb, who now is India's King.

Vaidya

It's our prayer
You'll be our saviour.

Dara

Not any more,
It's all over.

Hakim

Your noble son, Prince Sipihr, awaits you.
He hasn't moved from where his mother lies.
He's very quiet as he sits askew,
By her side. One hand he's placed on her eyes,
The other he's cupped into hers; his warm,
Hers cold; his red, hers marble. They are one
Become, like statues that come from Rome
Of lifeless Christ amd Mary. Except now it's *her* turn.

Dara

Take me to them, my friends.
All my life's meaning, ends.

SCENE XII

Inside Nadira's tent. Her bed is screened from view. Sipihr emerges from there, as Dara enters accompanied by others.

Sipihr

So it's all over, Father; she sleeps.
That last hour was Allah's pure gift.
No one, at such a going, weeps.
Her eyes were closed, though her hand could lift.

'My journey's over, my son,' she said,
Touching my fingers with gentle strength.
'But yours and your brother's lie ahead.'
I forbade her from speaking any length,
Much less words like those. But it was not
Mother speaking, it was a phantom.
She seemed of skies, not of earth, begot.
One for whom the firmament was home.

'It's time to go,' she turned and whispered,
*'Angels call me; they sing some strange text.
Their voices seem quite far and dispersed
One moment; as close as yours, the next.
'My mind sees all my past,'* she went on,
*'In one swift flash: my birth, youth,
Nuptials, motherhood, home and mansion,
Strife, battles, escape, exile—Life's truth.
I see all this from yon high mountain.
The music, son, is becoming loud.
I can see the fall of the curtain,
The readying of a purple shroud.
The music seems, quite strangely, white.
Odd, isn't it, for sound to show hues?*

And yet it's so: symphonies seem bright.
Colour every single wound, imbues.'

Then she said, *'There's a favour to ask:*
Your gentle sisters will need support.
You cannot fail me in this task,
Else they will lose faith in life's purport.
Promise me, you won't neglect them;
Our system does; it relegates us
–Women—to the role of garment's hem,
Folded, sewn-up, but continuous.
Keeping mankind's frayed edges rolled
With contrivance's needle and thread.'
I promised her that I would hold
My sisters' hands in mine, till they wed.

'Let me touch your head, son,' she then said,
Moving her hand towards me. *'Ah, there!*
I can hear coming from your head,
In the clearest tones, a prayer!'
I broke down and said I will fetch you,
But she said I should wait. *'He cannot*
Bear to see me go; you see we grew
Together. We've formed a tender knot.'

[*Sipihr is overcome*

Hakim

I asked the princess if she had instructions.
She opened her eyes, looked at me and said, *'Yes.*
You must not think I have pretentions
But, you see, I have never been homeless
Before. I die now in a wasteland,
A fugitive. What request can I make

Save this: inter me in Hindostan,
Beside a tranquil, lotus-bearing lake.'

Sipihr

She then closed her eyes and intoned, ever so soft,
'Alhamdu li'lahe Rab'ilalamin.' She had Will.
I wept in her hands, which had dried my tears so oft.
When I lifted my head next moment, all was still.

Dara

Still. All is still. Still this tent,
This night. Still my love, my life.

[Moving towards Nadira's body

And still I live, breathe, grow—why?
What a word! *Why.* Double you, aitch, vye.
There is more, much more, in that word's
Space than in all the world's
Vocabularies put together: Why.
Ask a pandit, mullah, pir, padre
Or fakir: Why, why all this, this birth
This death, this day, this night, this earth,
Sky, why you and me, why *Creation*?

They'll look at you with condescension:
'The man's mad: means well, poor fellow,
Give him a few years, he'll mellow.'
O Fates, why do you make and break,
What pleasure, in murder, do you take?
No artist does that to his work, unless
It be flawed. Nadira, were you not flawless?

ACT SIX

At Malik Jiwan's headquarters. Dara, coming to terms with his isolation, accepts an offer from the man who owes the prince his life.

SCENE I

Dara's soldiers are assembled under a tree. He addresses them, standing on a raised platform. He has aged almost overnight.

Dara

Sons, you have a free choice: Either with me to turn
Further westward to Persia for help or return
To your homes and hearths in beloved Hindostan
—Something which I will, most readily, understand.

A Soldier

Prince, do not think we are in a huff,
But we have had just about enough.

Other Soldiers

Yes, enough
Is enough.

First Soldier

Yet we sure wish you every good luck, prince.
Take us back, when you return, into your service.

Yes, we will join your service,
If—when—you are back, good prince.

Dara

We've broken bread together,
Drunk water from the same cup.
You have called me 'Father'.
But now my time is up.

Each soldier's a Sipihr
To me, I would you know.
Sipihr a plain soldier,
Though he be a Shukoh.

Dynasties are eyesores
Unless they have merit.
Thrones must be deserved; crowns
Are not hand-me-downs.

You've all done me proud,
In every single fight.
I will proclaim this loud:
You took on treason's might.

Now, as you return home,
Say this to those you meet:
Dara will never roam
Too far from Timur's seat.

Soldiers

Dara Shukoh Zindabad!
Aurangzeb Murdabad!

Dara

Don't murdabad my brother please.
Don't wish Aurangzeb's decease.
He may be a usurper,
But he's still my blood-brother.
Besides, he has not got me yet
And so you'd better save your bet!
Malik Jiwan Khan here
Is a good old friend.
Some time back he came near
Death—a most undeserved end.
Allah made me play a role
Although you might think this droll,
It's titled: 'Elephant's Tail'!
I will be his guest awhile
Here under his coolant roof
And plan my next fugitive mile.
Godspeed you, sons, on a fast hoof.

> *[The soldiers leave, saluting
> Dara. Many touch his feet*

Malik Jiwan

Come in, my prince, into my fort
So some mattes we can sort....

> *[Jiwan conducts Dara, Sipihr,
> Daud and Jester towards the
> building. As they are about to
> enter, ten soldiers of Jiwan's rush
> out and overpower Dara and the
> others*

Dara

Rascals! What are you trying?
Don't you dare touch me you knaves!

[*Looks at Jiwan who merely smiles*

Jiwan, is this your doing?
Is this how a host behaves?

Sipihr   [*Resisting with all his might*

You filthy curs,
You bloodsuckers,
Keep your hands off
You dirty sons of. . . .

[*A soldier pinions Sipihr and
ties his hands behind his back*

Jiwan

Fasten them tight;
To each other,
Prince, son, soldier—
And that sprite.

To Delhi they will go
And face the Emperor.

Dara

And *you!* You will face your Maker!
You faith-forsaker
You perfidious plotter,
You maggot-infested rotter!
Finish, finish, ungrateful wretch,

Finish, my life's luckless stretch.
We are victims, now immune,
To the blows of an evil fortune
And a brother's unjust passion.
Yet I'll make this admission:
If I now merit death
It is only for my faith
In the likes of Malik Jiwan
Who have my carriage driven
Straight, to the rim of my grave.

But remember: My son, brave,
Strong, has had his hands tied
Behind his back; no one's tried
Such an outrage on royal blood
Before. *Untie his hands, you clod!*

> *[Jiwan, after a moment's doubt,*
> *gestures to his men to unfasten*
> *Sipihr's hands*

SCENE II

Dara and Sipihr have been brought to Delhi by Jiwan in
fetters. They are ordered by Aurangzeb to be lodged in the
servants quarters of a mansion at Shahjehanabad, under the
wickedly watchful eye of Nazar Beg, a trusted slave of the new
king. Nazar Beg has an audience with Aurangzeb, in the
Diwan-i-Khas. Aurangzeb sits on Shah Jehan's throne. Dara's
seat has been removed.

Aurangzeb

Tell me: how do the 'princes' fare;
Do they talk ... or sit and stare?

Nazar Beg

Wildcats, the princes sometimes scream
But mostly, Lord, they daydream.

Aurangzeb

'Daydream?' you disgraceful wretch!
To dream they must be well indeed,
Well-fed, well-slept, free to stretch
Their limbs and minds in good meed.

Nazar Beg   [*Quailing*

Infidel father and insolent son
Fettered now have furled their pride
And in a rude stone dungeon
Like caged panthers curl and hide.
Lord of the Earth! Pray tell your slave
(Who kisses the dust your slippers tread)
Should their vault's dim architrave
Bats aside, hold greater dread?
Fanged millipedes I could release
Or taut-tailed scorpions, into that cell,
Tie the twosome to ant-crawling trees
And give them a foretaste of hell.

Aurangzeb

The Emperor's word gives contours;
It's you who must fill in the shades.
If but sharp minds, not senile boors
Comprised this 'Court of Pearls and Jades'
Would all my time on plans be spent
While the public's spleen on me is vent?
That's all I need say in firman!
So on with it. . . . But just a moment.

Tell the diligent Jiwan Khan
To take the infidels on elephant
Back, through every street and twisting gully
So to instruct the people of Delhi.

[*Nazar Beg withdraws*

SCENE III

*August 29, 1659, Chandni Chowk, Delhi's main market centre.
It is crowded with the city's anguished residents, rich and poor,
men and women. Father Busee, Manucci and Bernier stand on
a shop's balcony. They are watching Dara and Sipihr being
paraded through the city by Malik Jiwan Khan, as Aurangzeb
has ordered, on the back of a female elephant made repulsive
by a coat of slime. Women's wails and the sound of horses'
hooves are heard, together with the repetitive sound of the
elephant's bell.*

Blind Beggar

Dara Shukoh, prince of woe!
Prince of woe, Dara Shukoh!

Bernier

To rig up all this magnificence
—Swords drawn, bows taut with arrows—
Betrays a contorted malevolence.
Aurangzeb's mind, no one knows.

Busee

His uncanny sense, his 'touch', are sure.
But this graceless spectacle, this insult

To a much-loved prince with heart so pure
Will, in nameless miseries, result.

Manucci   *[The elephant bell sounds closer*

It is truly the most disgraceful
        Show I have ever seen
Dara, brave, noble, sagacious,
        Has through these alleys been
So often, counseling, listening, and
        To assist, so keen.

To take him now, thus broken and crushed,
        Through sites of his glory
Tells us of spite, of course, but also
        Of another story.
It tells us that Fate's favourite
        Reading, is Tragedy.

Mochi   *[Loud enough for Dara to hear*

Dara Shukoh, I'll nail his toe
When next I go, to shod your foe!

                              [Two cavalrymen 'escorting'
                              Dara enter, dismounted, with
                              lances pointed at the crowd

First Cavalryman

Khamosh! You lice-filled curs, stand back!
Or else your walnut heads I'll crack.

Thelawala   *[Moving menacingly with*
                                    Subziwala towards the two
                                    cavalrymen

O yeah? You sewer rat's offspring
Don't dare to point your lance at us!
You unwashed spittoon of the king
Don't dare you fling that glance at us!

Sabziwala

Out, you cawing crows;
Aurangzeb's bubos!

                                    [The cavalrymen disappear, to a
                                    great cheering by the crowd

Mochi

Dara looks like a crushed flower,
    Sipihr like a bud.
Aurangzeb's may be King but our
    Minds are made up:
Dara will rule our hearts, our soul
    As no one ever could.
Dara will enter Time's scrolls
    As Dara, the Good.

Manucci   *[To Bernier*

Babar was Babur The Brave,
Humayun: The-Very-Close-Shave;
Akbar, well, Akbar the Great,
Jehangir, why, the Luxuriate,
Shah Jehan, the Aesthete,
And Dara. . . .

Nur   *[Who sits directly beneath the balcony, without looking up*

Virtue's Defeat.

The Crowd

Dara Shukoh, Sipihr Shukoh!
Sipihr Shukoh, Dara Shukoh!

Blind Beggar

With what will I remember you?
I wish your noble face I knew!
Leave behind something for me
Even if a trifle it be.

Doodhwala

What can he give the beggar,
Dara's a fugitive.
Except what's on his figure,
He has nothing left to give.

Blind Beggar

Dara, please do not go
Without leaving a memento!

The Crowd

A memento, memento
From Prince Dara Shukoh!

[There is a lull. All sounds still

Mochi

He lifts his face,
Such infinite grace!

170

He raises his arm,
What studied calm!
He turns it round,
(There's not a sound!)
To lift his mantle
What a tantal!
He gives it a spin
And it is—in!

[Dara's shawl flung by him,
comes on to the stage and mantles
Blind Beggar. There is a roar of
acclamation

Busee

That was a benediction,
    No gift.
A spiritual action,
    God-kist.

[The procession moves away, as
can be told by the diminished
sound of hooves and elephant
bells. A disturbance, off stage,
ensues

Thelawala

A scuffle,
I notice,
They muffle
With finesse.

Blind Beggar

Who between,
Lout and Lean?

Thealawala

Neither.
It's either....

Manucci

The crowd's beating up Paanwala
—I know the wily fella—
For offering a *paan*
To Malik Jiwan Khan.

SCENE IV

*The following day at the Diwan-i-Khas. Aurangzeb is seated
on the throne. An assortment of noblemen and courtiers are
present. Jiwan and Nazar Beg stand near Aurangzeb.
Roshanara sits behind the alcove.*

Aurangzeb

So they turned violent.
And you were all silent.

> *[Some courtiers rise nervously in
> self-defence. Aurangzeb bids them
> be quiet*

There is no harm in that,
It's not always tit-for-tat.
It is good strategy
To let caulked energy

Steam-off in incidents
Of sudden violence.

I prefer a riot
To a grumbling quiet.
Quick to start, quick to end,
With no reports to send
On the whys and wherefores.
It's over; no therefores!

But this crowd's different.
It was irreverent.
Yet it must not be touched,
No houses should be searched
For those who rioted
And dung-missiles pelted
On Malik Jiwan Khan
(I believe he likes *paan*).

                    [*Jiwan smiles sheepishly*

Going back, it was wrong
I think to make one who's strong
Look sorry, victimized.
Losers are sympathized
With, by all Indians
In these dominions.

I'm no psychologist
Nor an Indologist
But this I sure know
Indians always crow
Over a bully's fall.
But the next moment, all
Is forgiven; he's down

You see! And the crown
Has passed to another,
Perhaps, bully's brother!

The question now's what next?
We must find a context
—Not *pre* text—(watch your thoughts
Expunge such words with dots)
To punish the ex-prince
And end this whole sequence.

Roshanara   [*Rising in the alcove*

Great King! I'll watch my words.
Dara and Sipihr rest.
They rest—please mark my words—
In peace, like angels blest.
They expect rebellion,
Popular uprisings,
A great pandemonium
In which all the Jai Singhs
And Jiwan Khans of life
Will be just brushed aside
And, after the great strife,
(When all of us will hide)
They will, finally, rise,
Proceed to the Red Fort
And from your soldiers prise
The keys to this great court.
I know this can't happen
But that is not the point.
People want it to happen
And *that* is the point.
Dara executed
May be more reputed

Than Dara imprisoned
And under-provisioned.
But more reputed—when?
A century, or ten,
After we are all gone!
Who thinks of night, at dawn?
The 'context' is simple—
Dara's an infidel.
Have him dubbed a heretic,
The rest is automatic.
Not under your title;
Make it sacerdotal.

SCENE V

A week later, in Dara's prison. Dara and Sipihr are seated, on the floor cooking their meal for fear of eating poisoned food. The date is August 30, 1659.

Dara

Lentils take long to boil;
But they do not spoil!
They will outlast today;
Will *I?* I cannot say.

Strange, do you not find it,
That I, who am to quit
Life any moment now
Should be so keen somehow

To avoid being poisoned.
I am inquisitioned:
'How did Sadullah die?
Can you your role, deny?'

God knows the role I played,
Who was by who, betrayed.
So this writer of books,
This brave fighter, now *cooks!*

What won't man do to live?
Anything but forgive,
I suppose, to postpone
Entering the Unknown.

I wanted a repast,
A rich dramatic cast
Of man, woman and beast,
Playing, God's eyes to feast.

[Moving the pot from the fire

But, by a divine switch,
(I first thought it a 'hitch')
Allah just shifted me.
Bodily lifted me.

From audience to stage
And said: 'Now go and wage
Your war, the last and best,
At Misfortune's behest.

'Put losers in your script,
They've lived in a closed crypt.
End their enforced silence,
And give them utterance.

'You have fought tragedy
In wars that were heady.
But now you must do more,
Become the hurtful sore!

'Don't be grief's pedestal,
Rather, its great symbol.
Noble in misfortune,
Verily, a tribune.

'For the world's failures,
Its blasted careers,
Undeserved vanquishments
Unexplained punishments.

'Become a synonym,
A dirge, a plangent hymn,
For unclever virtue
In its unrelieved rue.

'Rob triumph of stature
In honour's prefecture,
As a prince whose defeat
Made triumph counterfeit.'

When I saw this vision
Of my life's fruition,
My heart felt a great peace,
Unconcerned with life's lease.

[Serves the lentils into two earthen bowls

I now see Allah's will
In the course of my rill.
It sure has meandered
Flowed thin and gone under,

To but re-appear,
Pure, cool, crystal-clear,
My little destiny
Concerns epigoni.

A prince who will never
Be an 'ex' or a 'future'.
A prince, ever present,
Like a good Vice-Regent:

A promise of merit
You reach, not inherit.
A wisdom to be used
With humility, fused.

Princes trivialize
What they so greatly prize:
Their office, crown and throne.
That pattern, I disown.

By His switch in my role,
Allah has saved my soul.
I will always be seen
A forever might-have-been.

A promise, not regret,
No prince degenerate.
I will capsule men's hope
In humanity's scope.

They thought I eyed the crown.
I won't that taint disown.
But go a step ahead
And offer them—my head:

You said I sought the crown
So here, I've renounced.
Not just my crown—my head!'
Let Murder go ahead.

I think *that* sacrifice
The paying of that price

Will be a worthwhile stand
By a prince of Hindostan.

From our Holy Prophet
We have learnt the secret
Of being unafraid
Of injury or death.

We know Death is certain
And yet are so afraid
Of the falling curtain,
Our exit we degrade.

I'll go like a soldier,
But not resisting Death,
Nor hating the ogre
Who comes to still my breath.

Hereafter I'll prefix
All norms of succession
An inconvenient jynx
Who'll embarrass Ambition.

I hoped our monarchy
Would quickly terminate
Rule by oligarchy,
Justice inaugurate.

I thought Moghul rulers
Would, progressively, be
More than builders—healers,
With human sympathy.

Each Moghul advancing
His precursor's efforts
Some physic to bring
For India's deep hurts.

Her wars, her crimes, her hates
Her wrongs—man's doings, all—
Till our people's pain abates
And, together, we honour His call.

I just said 'our people'
Did I not? *Mark that phrase!*
In mosque and in temple
Dwells the Almighty's grace.

The Rab'ilalamin
Is everybody's !
A truth great Musalmin
—Unlike our court toadies—

Have known well, but, pity!
We've chosen, we Timurids,
To treat two out of three
Sons of Ind as mean hybrids,

Mongrel. Oh, how unwise,
And low! After Ghazni,
Ghori, who did not disguise
Their aim: Indian money,

And sped with sacks of loot,
We got the chance—a gift—
To take Gangetic root;
Not put down, instead, lift

India's sons and daughters
Into a Tree of Life
Where sky's dew, earth's waters,
Could nourish peace, end strife.

We got the chance to build
Great palaces in stone

But also more—to weld
Forts with huts poor folk own,

In a purpose so pure,
So selfless and true
As would of course ensure
Our line, but also hew

Trust out of suspicion,
And faith out of fear.
But no, cheap ambition
Cannot counsel hear,

The counsel of insight.
'Our people?' 'What on earth!'
Retorted Moghul might
In power-drunk mirth.

'We are here to rule
India's unwashed mob.
Dara's a bloody fool,
Meant but to sit and sob.'

But, son, they're mistaken
It is *they* who will grieve,
When forlorn, forsaken,
They run through history's sieve.

Run through they will, crown and clan,
Chortling into the void
For no other reason than
Their never having *tried*

To get under India's skin,
Inside her wondrous soul,
Never trying to win
Her trust, which is her all.

But I would not bemoan
The dying of a line,
So many, known, unknown
Have passed on just like mine.

What is truly tragic
Is we are ensuring
Our future will be sick,
Vengeful, unforgiving

Will hatch a reaction
Much worse than our action.
The future will pay
For the present's delay,

Its failure of role
To see, understand
India's textured whole
And stay Division's hand.

We were meant to unite
Those we have taught, now, to fight.
That is my true regret
The rest, my fate, I can forget.

Now, dying, let me intone
God's holy name, and own
I've sprung from the same earth
As any of mundane birth.

Like an eager rainbow
Let me to the sky go,
A vestibule of hues
Where hope and regret fuse.

Where pain and forgiveness,
Man's faith and faithlessness;

His desire for height
And, alas, this short sight.

The dead weight of life's tare—
All these—become Light; where
Man's instincts, no more savage,
With his Spirit, voyage.

Victory is heady,
But a true tragedy
Can serve humanity
For an eternity.

If I have served that purpose,
If I have made men feel
(As true tragedy does)
The hurt they did not heal

The gulf they did not close
The shame they did not share,
I'll go, Heaven knows,
Without a single care.

Kasi's Poet—Acharj
Living on Ganga's marge
Has with patience explained
What the *Geet* has ordained.

But we can wait no more
For those Descents of yore.
We must interiorize
The mercy of His eyes

A lot of pain there'll be
From snowmelt to sea.
Sickness contorts our land.
Sickness of the mind and

Sickness of the soul.
That's where I 'lost' my role.
A 'proper' succession
Or a 'smooth' transition,

My vanity had thought,
Would bring the rogues to naught.
I was myopic, wrong
To think myself so strong.

Or even deserving
Of the status of King.
My life will now end
Not story, but legend.

So I have no regret
(It's others who must fret).
As I prepare to go
To where, I think, I know.

But I will—must—admit
I cannot deny it
—I am wholly human—
I miss Sulaiman.

He was our House's hope,
Seen through Time's telescope
As the ace progeny
Redeeming epigoni.

With succession profaned,
Sulaiman's now orphaned.
Who knows what awaits him?
May Allah be with him.

And then there persists, yet
Another pang of regret:

Jester's disappeared:
Murdered, it is feared.

But I can't believe it:
He's such a free spirit!
I pray he's not in fetters,
Or that, in pain, suffers.

More faces come to mind:
Friends whom I leave behind.
Daud Khan the doughty,
And Firuz Mewati.

I can't forget Jaswant,
Once brave and valiant
Later by threats seduced
And in stature, reduced.

When I think great Sarmad
—Our living Talmud—
Is but four *kos* from here,
Angels I can hear.

A strange peace emanates
From him and permeates
My being. Mian Mir,
The unparalleled Pir

Had that effect on me.
Mian Mir beckons me.
As does your late mother,
And yes, my own mother.

Take care of your sisters,
And stay in touch with mine.
Kin should be banisters
To lean on the incline.

I hope they'll take you soon
To meet your grandfather.
In Aurangzeb's high noon,
He is a prisoner.

I now await beheading,
But why should *you* be finished?
It is I who was to be King.
Why should you too be punished?

> *[A sound of rusty padlocks being
> opened is heard. A very agitated
> Father Busee enters, followed by
> Nazar Beg who walks with
> calculated composure*

Father Busee! Are you alone?
No, you are not; you are not.
You have come with Death's clone;

> *[Turning to Nazar*

A very good likeness, you've got.
What weapon do you carry,
You poor little devil?
I see you will not tarry,
To do your bit of evil.

> *[Sipihr goes and clings to Dara*

Busee

I was told an hour back
To come and be with you;
Was told that this manjack
Has orders to. . . .

Dara

Execute me. Well, go on,
But don't you touch my son!

[Addressing Sipihr

Nazar Beg

Get up,
Pup!

[Incensed

Dara

You mongrel's eczema,
Perfidy's smegma,
Don't you dare berate
A ranking Prince of State!

Nazar Beg

Exceed not your limits,
You palm without digits.

Dara   *[Stunned by the insult but*
                  controlling his fury

Go tell my usurper
    Brother . . .

Nazar Beg

I am no message-bearer;
I am an executioner

                  [More soldiers enter. They tear
                  Sipihr from his father's clasp.

187

*Dara sends one, two, three
soldiers hurtling. There is a pause
in the grim scene*

Busee

My brief is brief,
I cannot stay.
And my grief . . .
I must pray
With you, prince
And since . . .

Dara   *[Touching Busee's shoulder,
                                      redemptively*

I will now pray in paradise
In the light of Allah's eyes.

Leave my son; just let him be.

                                     *[The father in Dara now tries a
                                      different gambit. He speaks
                                      moving towards the soldiers, one
                                      step forward with each sentence*

Not he, I, am your enemy.
He's still Prince, don't forget!
Your King's daughter he might wed.
Your King can get quite angry
You know; his temper's hungry.

Sipihr

Abbajan, take care!
They have a rapier!

> *[A screaming Sipihr is bundled*
> *out. The soldiers pounce on Dara*
> *who staggers but does not fall*

Dara

Hold it,
One minute,
I knew
Some of you.
Tell your king,
Dara kings him not!
He has loathing
For what Aurangzeb's got.
Because that is *not* Hindostan;
Certainly not its soul. . . .
But he will *never* understand.
Power, after all, was his only goal.

> *[Even as Sipihr's screams*
> *continue to be heard, the*
> *executioners overpower Dara and*
> *behead him*

ACT SEVEN

Shahjehanabad and its vicinity. News of the prince's execution has slouched into the city's alleys.

SCENE I

Later that evening in a ruin not far from the scene of Dara's execution. Jester hides amidst its crumbling walls. As he talks to himself, Jester keeps hearing Dara's voice.

Jester

What was it for,
This bloody war?

What did you prove?
That failures move?

That they uplift,
Are 'Heaven's gift'?

All that is crap,
Scented giftwrap,

For what is inside:
Fiasco's dead hide.

You have been licked.
(Don't you say *'tricked'*)

But not just you;
Virtue's virtue!

That's what's been trounced,
Its death, announced.

'Goodness can't pay,
Is what they'll say.

'Cleverness, does.
Don't think; see us!'

I won't agree,
I am zany.

Besides, I've loved you,
Soul and sinew.

But I remain
And you are slain.

You've been quartered
(Don't say *'martyred'*)

By Aurangzeb's
Grotesque slaves,

Twixt floor and wall.
I've heard it all.

Heard the story.
It is gory.

It's got you, prince,
Your awful jinx

By your throat,
Like a stoat.

Your story's dead
Before it's read.

Dara you're gone!
Will be reborn?

Dara you're dead!
I've lost my head?

Dara, you've quit!
I'm just a twit?

You're the forgotten.
Wool-of-cotton,

[Speaking at nonstop speed, so as not to be interrupted by 'Dara's voice'

The lint bandage
—Hurt's appendage—

Which the King tied
On injured pride

When, deflated,
Isolated,

He needed aid,
Found you prepared

To play that role.
—Heart and soul—

The role of sling
For supporting

His hand gone slack
From a hairline crack.

The limb's now dated,
Amputated,

Chucked with disdain
For human pain,

Bone, flesh and skin,
—Into the bin.

The king's no king,
God save his sling!

*[He collapses, exhausted by his
effort. After a moment, resumes,
contrite*

Dara, have I hurt you?
I will not continue.

Why are you so silent
When I've been violent?

Weren't you interrupting
And contradicting

Me a moment ago
Right here, on this floor?

Repeat that, please, my prince,
I can't endure silence.

Speak to me, Dara, speak,
I'm Jester, your pipsqueak!

Silence . . . of course, silence.
You're gone; crossed the Fence.

I was hallucinating.
You couldn't have been talking.

193

You are 'dead and gone'
Like all that's ever born.

If God is a Designer
You were, well, His error.

A defect in design,
To which men will resign.

After all, God's human
Not superhuman.

He was, perhaps, withdrawn.
Or to some problem drawn

When you lay on his Wheel
A dollop he could feel

Shape, elongate, reduce
According to the use

But forgot all about.
So you were taken out

Just as you'd shaped yourself
—Unfit for any shelf—

Except your very own,
Condemned to be alone.

In rigid seclusion,
To the exclusion

Of normal company,
Society's symphony.

'Dara is peerless,
Dara's sui generis!'

All right, so bloody what?
What has Peerless got?

A dagger on his neck,
His dream a ruddy wreck.

And where were you, great God
When your good Servant called?

He needed your succour,
Help from his Begetter,

In whom he placed such trust
As had *us* embarrassed

But no, you were busy
You sent Father Busee

(*Such* consideration.
Great commiseration!)

As your Special Envoy
—In Murder's own convoy!—

To tut-tut when the dread
Knife severed Dara's head.

Now *aren't* you quite pleased?
You have honoured the deceased.

And well you might conclude
—Stifling a yawn—'*Though rude,*

Dara's death's been condoled,
Mourned; well-handled, all told.'

But Mister just you wait,
Don't you try exculpate

Yourself in this grim tale
Or try your role, to veil.

Don't you see how justice
Is slain by injustice?

Goodness trapped, chained, butchered
By Evil and vultured

By Satan's avengers,
His hungry scavengers?

Do you not see all this?
What does your Book call this?

Are you completely blind
Or just out of your mind?

A not unnatural stage,
Perhaps, in one your age.

Will you tell me, Mister,
(Or. since you administer

Life and Death in sharp draughts).
Doctor God, sir, what crafts

Must human goodness learn
To your blessed favour, earn?

More fundamentally
I beg you, enlighten me:

You, who in virtue dwell
Do you govern Luck as well?

Or is Luck (Christ save us!)
Totally autonomous?

I am afraid she is
Or at least she perceives

Her smart self to be,
In ceaseless vanity.

Those whom you have fielded
Need, next, to be shielded.

But you're no good at that
So Luck issues her diktat.

While you just sit and stare,
Perhaps you do not care.

And so do not resist.
Perhaps you don't exist. . . .

How can he care or dare,
Doctor God's just not there!

Life's a suppurating bog,
Home of cur and filthy hog,

Other crawling fungi
Lidding deeper algae

Where cell-eats-cell-eats
Tissue-breeds-tissue-breeds. . . .

And in the shrink-expand
Of lymph, duct and gland

In the world's faecal bake,
This orgiastic lake,

What is Honour, Rectitude
And what is Ingratitude?

What has Virtue got to do
With a libidinous loo?

Never let thought travel
Life's truth to unravel.

Life is no Great Riddle
It's just a plain swindle!

Let us not rue Dara Shukoh;
He's gone the way all creatures go.

'Some go, their blood unspilled,
Some miserably killed.'

But *all* to the dungheap
On mushroom beds to sleep.

    Bravo!
    Bravo?

Did someone say bravo?
Surely not Dara Shukoh?

There! There we go again
On our favourite refrain:

'May be Dara exists,
Light in Darkness persists,

               [There is a flash of lightning

'May be God watches us,
Man and beast and fungus.'

Dara! when will doubting end
How long will you pretend

That I'm out of my senses
And these aren't coincidences?

> *[Another flash which alters Jester's tone*

I suppose ... there will be a doubt....
Till the last man goes out.

> *[A final burst of lighting is
> followed by the muezzin's call, a
> particularly soft, sublime call,
> which Jester hears with silent
> receptivity*

SCENE II

*That night, in the austere dwelling of Sarmad, the mystic. He
is seated on the floor, surrounded by devotees of all faiths.
Abhaichand, his disciple and 'host' enters.*

Abhaichand

Great Teacher, the deed is done;
Evil over Good has won.
Dara has been beheaded
Virtue wails; gleeful are the wicked.

His remains, bloody, disjointed,
Are to be paraded, flaunted,
By Aurangzeb's decree,
For the 'benefit' of Delhi.
And then interred without fuss
Near Emperor Humayun's.

Sarmad   *[After a pause*

Beheaded
Is God-headed.

Clouds part,
Reveal His Heart.

From its throne,
The peacock has flown.

SCENE III

*The Diwan-i-Khas, after some weeks. The Moghul Emperor
Aurangzeb is about to enter. Heralds—Third and Fourth—
await him. The ladies' alcove is unoccupied.*

Third Herald

Who are the King's visitors today?
Does something fresh come our way?

Fourth Herald

There is Mir Jumla's proposition
    For Sarmad's execution.
And we have old Tavernier, bringing a new jewel.
Business Is As Usual.

            *[Taking out a necklace from his
            inner pocket—a brand new
            present from the French
            merchant*

Excerpt from

SARMAD SHAHEED

An essay written by
MAULANA AZAD

*In 1910—a hundred years before this publication
(Translated by Syeda Saiyidain Hameed and published
by the Indian Council for Cultural Relations,
New Delhi, 1991)*

During the last days of Emperor Shahjehan, Dara Shikoh
was heir-apparent. A man of Sufi temperament, he was
unique among Mughal princes. It is a blot on historical
veracity, that the pen which recorded the history of the
Mughal period was always held by Prince Dara Shikoh's
enemies. Behind the screen of political manoeuvres, the
real picture has become blurred. Form his early years
Dara displayed the attributes of a Dervish. He always
kept company with philosophers and sufis. His writings
indicate that the author was a man of excellent taste. The
overwhelming proof of his taste is that in pursuing his
goal he lost the distinction between the temple and the
mosque. The humility with which he met the Muslim
divines was matched by the devotion with which he
bowed his head before the Hindu saints and sadhus. Who
can deny the purity of this principle?